3

REIGNING ASCENT

The Pearson Prophecy, Book Three

JEN L. GREY

REIGNING ASCENT
JEN L. GREY
COPYRIGHT © 2018

Proofread by Jamie Holmes

Edited by Kendra Gaither

Cover Design Eden Elements Publishing

To my readers that have continued this journey with me, thank you so much.

Chapter One

I stand by the old, worn carriage, trying to believe what my eyes are seeing. Not ten feet away is my brother who I haven't seen for a year.

Surrounded by forest, we are about thirty minutes away from the Noslon village. It's disconcerting, because it's spring, and the forest should be in full bloom, but it looks like it could be mid-winter. The trees are bare, and there are no scents of blossoming flowers in the air. Granted, there is a chill this early morning, but that's not unusual in this part of Knova.

Owen, Jacob, Mer, Willow, and I are on our way back to Agrolon, and the carriage had stopped, which made Owen want to investigate. However, he can't go anywhere without me.

With a long beard and messy, black hair, Logan looks as if he's been out in the woods for a while. He has dark circles under his eyes, and the whites around his pupils are tinged with red.

Owen, my soulmate, is getting upset. His breathing is shallow, his fist clenched. "I asked what the problem was and expect an answer."

Focusing on me, my brother ignores him and moves in my direction.

Mistaking the situation and feeling that I'm being threatened, Owen jumps in front of me.

Logan looks past him to meet my eyes. "Is it really you?"

He has thought I was dead all this time. I don't blame him for second-guessing. I nod and hold my hand out.

He shoves Owen. "Get out of my way."

This will not turn out well. My brother is just processing that I'm alive. However, my mate is worried that he might be someone who used to mistreat me.

"You aren't going anywhere near her. She belongs to me and is under my protection," Owen growls, pulling him away from me. He pushes Logan's back against a tree. His demeanor seems cool, but rage is bubbling through our bond.

Scowling, Logan lifts his chin. "Like hell she is."

If I don't step in, things are going to escalate. I pull Owen off him. "Both of you, just calm down. Owen, this is Logan, my brother."

I turn and reach out to my mate.

He relaxes under my touch, and his power ebbs. "Why didn't you just say that?"

I shrug. "I wasn't expecting to run into him so soon. It left me a little off-kilter."

Logan watches our interaction, concern outlining his face. "Who is this?" He points to Owen.

"This is my…" Whoa, I've never had to address this before. I can't really throw out soulmate right now. We need to ease into that. I glance to my mate, hoping for some help.

However, he takes a few steps back and leans against a tree, smiling.

Great, he's leaving me to flounder, and I can tell he is enjoying watching me try to explain our relationship. I'll remember this.

Grabbing my hand, Logan turns my attention back to him. "Has he been mean to you?"

"Oh, no. Not at all. He's my…" I trail off, trying to find the words.

His grip tightens. "Then why can't you finish your statement?"

Crap. He's right. I glance down, and my engagement ring comes into view. I tend to forget this since what we have is stronger than marriage. But, for right now, that's an easier explanation. "He's my fiancé."

Logan scratches at his scraggly beard.

How long has he been out here? He looks rough, and he doesn't smell much better than he looks.

He runs his hand over his face and glances back at me. He walks toward me and pulls me into a hug.

Desperate to know his feelings, I open our bond for the first time in over a year. As soon as I do, I wish I hadn't. His happiness, pain, anger, and confusion all slam into me at once.

He puts his lips to my ear. "Don't you ever do anything like that again."

Thank Knova he is going to let it drop for now. We

have more important things to focus on at the moment. The Agrolon guards are looking for the King of Noslon, and my mate is right here, ready to return with them.

I'm sure they've been expecting his father, but Owen has been in charge since he was young. Due to the greedy kingdoms surrounding them, his mother was fortunately strong with power and was able to create a barrier around Noslon to keep their people hidden. She knew that either the Agrolon or Orlon King would try to take over during their time of turmoil.

My brother marches over to Owen. "Who are you, and where do you think you're going?"

Smirking, Owen stands from the tree. "I'm the King of Noslon, and I'm traveling to your kingdom as requested."

Anger flashes across his face. "And you think it's wise and safe to take your...," he glances back at me and clears his throat, "fiancée with you?"

This is not going well. My brother does not want me going back to the unsafety in Agrolon, and Owen won't tolerate being questioned by an outsider.

Owen motions toward me. "Why wouldn't it be? She's the perfect distraction."

I wish he would not come off as a jerk to my brother. Yes, King Percy and Princess Elizabeth hate me since I'm not the Savior, but he doesn't want to use me as a distraction. He's just pissed that he's being challenged.

Raising an eyebrow, Logan smirks. "Oh, you mean with the two princes?"

They do realize we have more pressing things going on, right? This whole thing is getting ridiculous. And what does he mean by the two princes? Does that mean Sam is there, too?

Owen's face slips for just a minute. "Look, are we going to stand here, or do we want to get going?"

"Why don't you go back to the village and leave your party behind?" Logan glances at me. "Do we really need to drag innocents into this?"

That pisses me off. He still thinks I'm the same girl who lived in the palace in fear. I'm not that naïve anymore, and he better damn well catch up. I place my hands on my hips. "Too bad there aren't any innocents to drop off."

Scowling, he takes a step toward me. "What does that mean?"

"Take it however you want, but where he goes," I point to Owen, "I go."

A young Agrolon guard walks up. "Sir, is there a problem?"

He lets out a sigh. "No, not at all." He points over to my mate. "This is the new King of Noslon. It's time to go home."

The Agrolon troops rally, working to get everyone situated for the ride.

Taking my hand, Owen steps close to me. *You know, you could have told me he was your brother.*

I always forget that we can mind-speak. I glance at him. *I'm sorry. I forget that we can do this. Be nice, he's hurting.*

He cuts his eyes over to me. *How do you know?*

I ignore him and walk ahead. I'm not ready to reveal our bond just yet.

He snickers. "You do realize that doesn't give you an excuse not to answer?"

I turn around and stick out my tongue.

Ares trots into view. "Hey, boy, how are you?" I reach up and pet him.

"It's so weird that he lets you get close to him. He lets Mer, but it took her about five years of bribing him to allow it. He is still skittish around her." Owen scratches his head. "Come on, let's get back in the carriage."

Ares stomps, blocking me.

The last time he did this, he wanted to give me a ride. That is a nice alternative. The carriage is made for four, but that's with no personal space, so we are all crammed in there. I walk over to mount him, and he doesn't complain.

Owen's mouth is hanging open.

"What's wrong?"

He closes his mouth. "I know he let you on his back when you drained yourself that day in the forest, but I thought that was just because of the situation. He doesn't let anyone ride him, that I know of. It's strange. I wonder if he'd let us ride together?"

I shrug. "We can try."

He walks up to Ares with his hands in the air.

Yeah, that makes you look so innocent.

When he is within two feet of Ares, the stallion startles back.

I pet his neck and lean down to whisper close to his ear, "Can Owen ride, too?"

The stallion stomps but stops backing away.

Owen takes a few steps, reaching Ares, and extends his

arm. After a few minutes, he must take it as a good sign, so he walks closer and mounts behind me.

"Uh, why aren't you in front?" I turn to face him.

He grins. "Because I wouldn't be able to do this." He wraps his arms around me, pulling me flush against him. Our powers merge, and I relax back into him, enjoying his touch.

The guards up ahead move, excitement brimming. They had their tents packed up within minutes, eager to get home.

We follow behind them, riding alongside the carriage.

"So, that's your brother, huh?" Owen leans forward to speak into my ear.

"Yes, but I'm not sure he's too thrilled to see me."

He runs his fingers along my sides. "You know that's not true. He is ecstatic but doesn't want you going back to Agrolon. To be honest, I'm not thrilled about it either."

Truthfully, neither am I, but we don't have much of a choice. Our land is dying and we need to figure out what's going on. If the West is rising and the cause of this destruction, we must face them head-on. Even if we tried to hide, the West would come looking for us eventually.

I tilt my head so that I'm looking back at him. "Where you go, I go. We're one now. How would you feel if I tried to leave you behind?"

His eyes flash. "Never would happen."

I never believed I would find my soulmate when I ran from Orlon. I figured I would be alone for the rest of my life. But I found my way to Noslon, and despite us both fighting it, we found one another. Our matching tattoos that appeared when our bond formed confirmed it all.

"Remember, we're supposed to fight our own battles? When did that change?"

His hands tighten their hold on my waist. "The moment I gave my heart to you. I may have fought it, princess, but no more. You are mine to protect."

My heart flutters at his words. I don't get tired of them, but even if he wants to protect me, I can't hide forever in Noslon. A war is coming, and even if I'm not the Savior, I have a part in it. I just hope I'm ready to face my demons, because tomorrow, I'll be staring right at them.

My hands get clammy and my stomach revolts. Flashes of the king pushing me off that balcony, the way Nick looked at me the last time, and Sam backstabbing me flash through my mind. Am I strong enough to face them? Should I have fought and tried to keep us back at Noslon?

Logan glances back at me.

Crap, our bond is open.

Before I can react, Owen kisses my neck. "I'm sorry. I didn't mean to make you doubt yourself. You're right, this is your battle, but we will face it together. You and me, forever."

His encouragement is all I need. We are in this together, and those traitors should be prepared.

❧❧

DUSK IS FALLING AND THE SUN IS SETTING. WE'VE BEEN traveling most of the day with very few stops. We came upon a semi-level spot where a small stream is located just a few feet away. The trees are browner here, and the chill in the air is crisper.

We're all hurrying to set up camp. My body is sore from all the riding we've done. That's what happens when you live in a village for a year and don't have to travel long distances. Tomorrow morning is going to hurt.

The carriage stops with a racket. It's large and made of dark wood, but it makes a lot of noise since it hasn't been used in over ten years.

Mer stumbles out of the carriage, her black hair sticking up in the back. Her jade eyes, the same color as her brother's, meet mine. "My goodness, I think my legs are asleep. How long were we in that thing?"

She is being dramatic again. Noslons aren't used to being cooped up like that. So, even though there was plenty of room, she is still miserable.

"Hey, at least you had room. Imagine if Owen and I had joined you all." I stretch out and try to ease some of the soreness from my legs and backside.

Walking up behind me, Owen massages my shoulders.

I moan, leaning into him.

Jacob squeezes out of the carriage, his hulky form almost too large for the hole. His blue eyes assess the area.

I would expect nothing less of my mate's best friend.

Willow pokes her head out from the carriage, and Jacob hurries over and grabs her hand, helping her out.

"Hey, why didn't you help me?" Mer crosses her arms.

He pivots her way. "Because someone was pushing everyone out of the way so they could be the first one out."

I laugh.

Groaning, she looks at the sky. "If you hadn't been taking forever, then we wouldn't have had a problem."

"Then don't blame me for not helping you. Obviously, you were more concerned to get out." He rolls his eyes.

Logan heads over and stares me down. "As much as I hate to interrupt this riveting conversation, I would like to speak to my sister."

I nod and head toward my brother, Owen right on my heels.

Logan scowls in his direction and crosses his arms. "I want to speak to her. Alone."

Wrapping an arm around me, Owen pulls me against him. "Where she goes, I go."

Great. They are in a peeing contest. As much as I love my brother, Owen is my other half. I can't dismiss him at this point, or it will diminish his importance to me.

The veins on Logan's neck bulge. "Like hell…"

I raise my hand, cutting him off.

"He's right. He and I are a package deal." I reach for his arm. "Whatever you have to say to me can be said in front of him."

Owen rubs my arm where my matching tattoo is hidden under my shirt.

I'll never forget the day they formed. It was the first day we agreed to give our relationship a chance. We went for training, and his mother asked us to merge our powers. When we did, it was amazing and our matching tattoos appeared. They are a thorn design similar to the family key I wear around my neck.

The night we cemented our bond, the same design

appeared on our wrists with thorns connecting them to the one on our arms.

Hurt etches into Logan's face. He takes a deep breath and looks away. "Fine."

Turning to face the rest of our party, Owen looks at each one. "Go help the guards set up camp. We pull our weight. Do you understand?"

Jacob nods, but Willow just smirks.

My brother walks off into the woods, and Owen and I follow behind him.

After we are a good distance away from the others, Logan turns to me. "Where the hell have you been?" His tone is rough with emotion. "The king swore you were dead."

Needing to connect, I walk over to him.

He pulls me into his arms.

"The king pushed me over the balcony, and Sam helped me escape." I bury my face in his chest. "I've missed you so much."

"I've missed you, too. We all went crazy when they king told us you were dead. I knew you weren't, but Mother thought I was crazy." He pulls me in tighter.

Tears fall from my face. Having my brother here is something I thought would not be a possibility again. Some of the void that had been in my heart disappears. After a few minutes, I remember that Owen is nearby and pull away.

Wiping his cheeks, Logan takes a deep breath.

Owen comes up next to me and takes my hand.

Glaring, my brother looks in his direction. "If you left with Prince Samuel, how'd you wind up with him?"

I smile and my gaze lands on Owen. "Fate. I found the village and then, when I needed a home the most, Mer found me and brought me to Noslon."

Smiling, Owen bends down to kiss my lips.

Logan clears his throat. "Look, can we talk alone?"

Owen stiffens at the question.

I steady myself. *If you're not okay with it, I won't.*

Owen licks his lips. *He's your brother. Of course it's okay. If I thought Mer had been dead for the past year, I'd want some answers, too. However, I'm not going far and will be back in a few minutes. Let me know if you need me.*

I smile at him. *He's my brother. I'll be fine.*

Cracking his knuckles, Logan is tense and looking off in the other direction.

Moving back toward camp, Owen nods. "I'll give you two some space. I'll be back shortly."

Logan huffs and I smile reassuringly. Logan and I both watch Owen walk away.

After a moment of silence, Logan turns to me. "What the hell are you doing? He's a barbarian." He puts his hand on his forehead.

I laugh. "No, he's not. You don't know him."

"And you do? How well did you know Prince Nicholas and Prince Samuel? Don't be stupid."

That was below the belt. How dare he question me when he doesn't know the whole story. "Yes, I do. And you're right, but I learned my lesson from those cowards. Owen stood up for me in front of his own village. That's something neither one of those princes would ever do. At this point, I know him better than I know you."

Logan jerks back like he's been slapped. "What is

wrong with you? How could you say that? You're my sister, for crying out loud."

"Just because I'm your sister doesn't mean you can stand there and insult me. I've been through hell this past year, and I'll be damned if I'll have someone question my judgment. Our conversation is over if this is how it's going to keep going." I put my hands on my hips, glaring.

Within seconds, Owen is back at my side. He frowns at Logan and takes my hand, tugging me toward him. "Are you done?"

Logan takes a step toward him. "No, we aren't. You can go away again."

I turn my back to him. "You're wrong. We are done. This conversation is over. Nothing good will come of it. Come on, Owen, let's get back to the others." The two of us head back, leaving my angry brother behind.

I can't believe he is treating me like this when he hasn't seen me in forever. I always hoped we would have a happy reunion, but I should have known. "He's a jerk."

"Calm down. He is right to be concerned."

My eyes widen. "You're standing up for him?" I stop and stab my finger in his chest.

He chuckles and grabs my offending finger, lowering it to my side. "No, but I can respect his concerns. At one time, you were gullible."

What is this, jump on Ari day? "Don't you start, too. You'll be sleeping alone in that tent if you keep it up."

Owen grins wide and places his mouth on mine.

I try to pull away, but he doesn't let me. My mind grows hazy, and I forget why I was upset to begin with. Jerk. His kisses are pure bliss, especially when our powers merge to connect our souls. I'm so immersed in him that I don't hear someone approach.

"Are you serious?" Logan is glowering in our direction.

It breaks the spell and I pull back. Did my brother just catch me making out?

"Oh, that's normal." Mer walks toward us. "I would say that you get used to it, but 'immune' is a better word. They've been like this for a whole year, and it's getting worse."

I glance in her direction. Why does she show up at the most inconvenient times? "Remember, boundaries? Most of the time, it's because you just walk into our home uninvited."

Logan's jaw tenses. "What do you mean, your home? Do you live together?"

Crap, how could I let something like that slip?

Glaring at his sister, Owen growls. "For the love of Noslon, will you shut your mouth for once."

Pouting, Mer points at me. "Hey, she said it, not me."

"You live with him?" Logan stares at Owen. His anger is rolling off him. "You said fiancé. You're letting your reputation be soiled."

Even though he's being a jerk, I can understand why he's upset. This is bad, and I don't want him to think ill of me. I guess it's time to let him in on everything. I raise my hands. "We're more committed than marriage could ever make us."

"Have you lost it? It's like I don't know you."

Wow, the blows keep on coming. Well, I will just have to prove myself to him. I yank my jacket off and turn to Owen. *Take off your shirt.*

He looks over at me and gives me a naughty smile.

I glare at him. I'm not in the mood for his inappropriate joking.

He chuckles. "All right..." He removes his jacket and hangs it on a tree limb.

Confusion is etched all over Logan's face. "Have you both lost your damn mind?"

The cold wind is whipping around my body, and a shiver runs through me. Let's get this over with. "Look, we're soulmates."

Owen walks over to me, and we turn our arms so the tattoos are facing the same way.

Logan takes in our matching tattoos. He sucks in a sharp breath and stumbles back several steps. "That's impossible. Only the Originals had soulmates."

Why can't he just trust me? Yes, I made some poor decisions in the past, but boy have I learned. Nobody is more aware of that than me. "Well, not anymore. He's it for me."

Logan must sense my feelings, because he comes over and wraps his arms around me. "I'm so sorry. I know I'm being a jerk, but I just found you. It's amazing and I'm not handling it well. Look, I'm not thrilled about this, but if you're soulmates, well, that's it. Let's get back, eat some dinner, and get a good night's rest. We are close to the palace and should get there tomorrow evening if we make good time."

My stomach sours, but I try to ignore it. This is something I have to do, so why is it so hard?

Owen reaches out and touches my shoulder.

I glance up at him.

Giving me a small smile, he leans forward. "In it together, baby."

I nod back and take his hand.

Logan leads the way to the fire, and we all sit around together.

In the middle of the campsite, Willow is sitting cross-legged and smiles at our entry.

The other guards are standing on the other side of the fire that has been lit, so Owen heads over to them.

Taking a seat next to Willow, I let out a big sigh. This day has been more traumatic than expected.

She reaches over and puts her hand on my leg. "Are you okay?"

I sigh and pull my knees to my chest, wrapping my arm around them. "Is facing your demons ever fun?"

She squeezes my arm. "You are stronger than you realize, and although it won't be fun, you'll find some peace. Your heart will guide you, and your wisdom will keep you from repeating the mistakes from your past. Remember, you aren't the same person you were a year and a half ago. You've found yourself, and that's something you should be proud of. Your past made you who you are, so don't be ashamed of it. Embrace it and maybe... cause a little hell."

I smirk and lean into her side. "I'm so glad I found you all. Even though I've missed my family, I found my home. It's always been at Noslon."

Willow puts her arm around me. "I'm glad I found another strong daughter. You make our village better and my son happy."

Having someone so supportive in life is nice. I can't imagine my world now without her. We've grown close over the past year, and she is like another mother to me. "I love you."

Walking toward us, Mer pouts and sits down on the other side of me, taking my hand. "Oh, you're trying to become my mother's favorite, too?"

I place my hand over my heart. "Yes, my goal is to make sure I'm favored by everyone."

Owen heads back over and motions for his sister to move.

She glares up at him and scoots closer to me.

He bends, getting in front of her face. "Move. You're in my spot."

She flips her hair back. "I don't see your name on it."

"I think the tattoo you're leaning against says otherwise. Now, get up." He picks her up and sets her to the side, making room for him. He plops down beside me and takes my hand. "I leave you for one second, and I lose my spot."

I lean my head on his shoulder. "Well, that's what you get for leaving me."

"I'd never leave you. I was just five feet away."

I tilt my head up. "Felt like further to me."

Grinning, he leans down and kisses my lips.

We've been like this for over six months now, and I crave him more each day. I doubt this closeness will ever change or get old. I tend to lose myself in him.

He deepens our kiss and pulls me closer.

Someone pulls us apart.

I pull back and find myself uncomfortably close to Mer's face.

She points at us. "For the love of all that's holy, can you please stop doing that?"

You can always count on her to ruin our intimate times. I glance up and find that a young guard is trying to pretend he wasn't paying us any attention, and another guard is grinning right at me. Oh, dear goodness. Everyone got a show.

Logan is glaring. "Yes, we really don't want to be watching that."

I look down at my shoes, praying that when I look up everyone will be gone.

Owen puts his finger under my chin, lifting my head. "I love you."

My heart races, and I smile back. "I love you, too."

Jacob covers his head with his hands and groans. "I think you just made it worse."

Willow gets up, chuckling. "Well, now that we know they love one another, how about we eat before we get another show. Those two will be back at it soon if we don't get them preoccupied."

Despite his flinch, Logan turns to the other guards. "Go grab some food for everyone. It's getting dark, and we need to get some sleep."

Jacob stands and grabs Mer's hand, pulling her up. "Let's go help them and finish setting up our tents."

She looks at him conspiringly. "Is this so they can chat alone?"

Putting his hand over her mouth, he chuckles. "Just, sometimes, be quiet. We do need to finish setting up."

Yeah, that's not going to work. What is he thinking? All he's doing is encouraging her.

Giggling, she bites him. "That's what you get."

Jerking back, he looks at his hand. There is a bite mark on his palm. "Damn it." He shakes his hand and sighs. "Just, come on."

Grabbing her hand, Willow pulls her, following the guards. "Children, come on. We have work to do."

That's the thing about Mer. She is herself even when we are in a tense situation. She may annoy me sometimes, but life would be boring without her.

My brother comes over to me and sits in Willow's vacant spot.

I turn toward him and lean my back on Owen's chest.

Owen puts his arms around me, bringing me closer.

Snuggling in to his side, I'm ready to find out what I've wondered for a while. "How are Claire and Mother?"

He rubs his hands against his beard once again. "They're both good, but Mother has been a little crazy since you… uh… died."

I cringe. "What happened?"

Owen moves his hands and rubs my shoulders.

Shifting, Logan crosses his legs and stares at the fire. "Well, you left that morning with Princess Elizabeth, and Mother came into my room to wake me. She explained that you had been requested to walk with that awful person before the sun even rose, so we knew something was up. I got dressed and went to find you. I figured you'd be walking around the palace, or maybe in the garden, but I couldn't find you anywhere."

Of course, he wouldn't go looking for me at the royal chambers. We weren't allowed to go there. That's the one place no one but royalty and their elite guards are allowed.

He barks out a laugh. "I even went out to the stables. Like the princess would ever go there, but you weren't anywhere else. Where did you all go?"

Owen stills.

He's been wanting to hear this story, and each time he brings it up, I get him distracted. It's time to tell what happened and, maybe, I can tell it just once. "She took me to the royal chambers."

Logan's eyes widen.

However, I just need to get it all out. If I'm going to tell this story, I want it out. "When I got up there, she asked me if I thought they were stupid. After the scene both princes caused in our quarters, Dave ran right to Elizabeth and told her everything."

His jaw clenches. His fury at Dave's betrayal is evident. "Are you serious?"

I hold up my hand, silencing him. "Yes. The king came out and accused me of all kinds of things. He... well... he slapped me, hard, and then Nick ran out, telling him to leave me alone and that he loved me." The whole day returns to me, and for once, I'm angry, not hurt. Why do the king and princess think they have the right to treat someone so poorly? What are they so afraid of to make them that cruel?

Owen's arm around me tightens. His tone is deep, angry. "The king slapped you, princess?"

I wince at the raw hatred in his voice. "Do you want me to continue? I just need to get this out, please."

They both become silent.

"The king pushed Nick down and started kicking him in the ribs. He dragged him into a room and told Elizabeth to deal with me. She threw some kind of powder on me."

The memory is still fresh in my mind. I remember the hateful look on Elizabeth's face, how wild her dark red hair was. "I don't know what it was, but it reduced my power considerably. She tried to tie me up, but I managed to kick her away and tried to escape. However, she used her power and, honestly, I didn't have a chance. She tied me up in the room and left me."

Logan stands up and paces. The veins of his neck are bulging.

Raw power is flowing out of Owen, turbulent and volatile.

They are both angry, and now, I am, too. However, I'm angrier with myself. How could I have let them treat me like that? "After a while, I managed to untie myself, but then Nick walked through the door. Oh, I was so stupid. I thought he had come to save me." I laugh, the betrayal clear.

Logan opens his mouth.

But I hold my hand out. "If I stop, I won't finish."

Closing his mouth, my brother kicks the ground.

Owen's rage is overwhelming. He's still, but our bond lets me see what's going on in his head.

My whole body is shaking as I relive the moment. I take a deep breath, trying to calm my nerves. "He took me out to the royal balcony and told me that we were done, that he was marrying Emerson. He was going to say something else, but the king appeared and tossed me over the balcony. Luckily, Lydia was down below. She used her powers to save me. I would have landed on the jagged rocks and been washed out to sea otherwise. I would have died if she hadn't been there."

His arm trembling with anger, Owen's rage is about to break free. "This is the way you were treated at Agrolon?"

I close my eyes, knowing this is the calm before the storm of his fury. "Yes, it was. That's why I never wanted to discuss it. What good could it do?"

He releases my waist and stands. "Well, for one, we wouldn't be on our way to the freaking Agrolon Kingdom. But... we are. And there will be hell to pay."

No matter what, we have to go to Agrolon. He knows this. "You said yourself, we have to go. It's for the fate of all of Knova."

He pulls me into his arms and turns my head to the side, so I can see him. His eyes bore into me. "You are the most important thing to me. To hell with Knova."

I reach out and touch his face, running my thumb along his jawline. "I love you, but what about our village? The children? All the innocents everywhere? How I was treated in the past..."

"You're right." He places his forehead against mine. "But you better damn well be treated with respect or they will have to answer to me."

Leaning against a tree, Logan has been silent, watching our exchange. He pushes off and stands next to us, staring at me. "How'd you get out?"

I lick my lips and wiggle a little so Owen releases his grip. "Well, Lydia softened my fall. We hid from the guards, and then she took me to the back entrance of the castle where Hazel and Sam were." I take a deep breath. "Hazel had found Sam and somehow convinced him to come out there with her. As soon as he saw me, he fetched a guard. Within minutes, we were rolling out of the gates. He took me to Orlon."

The guards and the rest of our crew head back over.

The young guard hands out some food, and an awkward silence hangs in the air.

As we all eat our small rations, I can tell that even Mer is affected.

This day has been more stressful than expected. My eyes are drooping, and I'm struggling to keep them open. As soon as I'm finished eating, I stand. "I'm going to go put the tents together. I'm exhausted."

The young guard smiles at me. "Oh, you don't have to worry about that. It's already done. It's just right over there, where we came from."

How did they manage to do that? Have they been out here that long? I guess my conversations with everyone took longer than I realized. "Okay, thanks... uh... what's your name?"

The guard seems ecstatic. "I'm William. Please, let me know if you need anything."

Owen jumps up and takes my hand. "Come on, let's go."

We make our way past the group, heading to the tents. After a few feet, footsteps are behind us.

I turn and find Logan right there. "Are you ckay?"

"Yeah, just wanted to make sure you got to your tent okay." He points to one of the tents on the end. "You can stay in mine."

Owen shifts beside me, not pleased with the suggestion.

There is no way we'll be separated tonight. After the day we've had, I need his warmth and support. However, I don't want to hurt my brother's feelings. "Thanks, but I'm going to be staying with my party. The guards don't realize I'm your sister yet, so that might cause even more of a scene."

We turn when there is some rustling coming in our direction and find William making his way toward us.

He looks at my brother. "Do you need any help? You got up in a hurry, so I just wanted to check." He glances to us and looks at me and then back at him. "You know... I just realized that she looks a lot like you. That's crazy, right?"

Oh, this isn't good. We don't want the king alerted about our presence ahead of time. Nothing good would come out of it if he were to find out that I'm alive before we even make it back to the kingdom. The longer I can go without people recognizing me, the better. "Yes, it is. Goodnight."

I grab Owen's hand and head toward our tent.

When we walk into our tent, Owen flips me around to face him. His lips are on mine and we lose ourselves to one another.

Chapter Two

Sounds of people moving around outside has me waking, my eyes opening. I open my eyes and realize that Owen's already alert. "Why didn't you wake me?"

He grins at me and kisses my lips. "We have a big day ahead of us, and I wanted you to get your rest."

I do not want to leave this place, especially with the knowledge that we should arrive at Agrolon today. I smile and snuggle closer. "Can we just stay here?"

His chest shakes with laughter. "I would love to, but I'm surprised you made it this long. All that noise you hear is from your brother pacing outside our tent. He's not thrilled about us being in here together."

I tense. What does he mean? Was I so out of it that he has already been in the tent without me waking? "How do you know it's him?"

"Because that young guard from last night keeps trying to talk to him."

I kiss his lips and pull away, standing. I slept in my clothes, so I change into some clean ones and redo my braid. I glance over and realize Owen is watching me. "Everything okay?"

He smiles and walks over, kissing me once more. "Everything is perfect. You're so beautiful, inside and out. I'm so glad you're mine."

It's still amazing to me that this man loves me. I don't know what would have ever become of me if I hadn't met him. I wink at him. "Well, you're not so bad yourself."

"Ari…" My brother is outside our tent.

I roll my eyes, dreading his overreaction.

Owen smiles wider and motions toward the door.

I open the tent's flap and peek out. "Logan…"

He rushes over to me. "It's about time you came out. What took so long? Never mind… I don't want to know." He attempts to look around but settles his attention back on me. "We need to get moving. You better prepare yourself for what the day will bring. Are you sure you know what you're doing? You still have time to change your mind."

He acts as if I don't realize this. Does he not think I know that I'm about to face my past? Memories flash through my mind of the king's abuse and Elizabeth's cruelty. But for once, anger fills me and not pain. I can't believe I let them treat me like that. How had I been such a coward? I'm not the same person I used to be, and thank goodness. Why shouldn't they know that?

Touching my shoulder, he leans down. "Are you okay? See, this is why you need to turn around. I don't like the idea of you with him," he points inside the tent, "but at least there, you are safe from them."

Owen walks out of the tent and stands beside me. He wraps his arm around my waist. *We can go home, but you will regret it if you do.*

I suck in a deep breath and bite my lip. He's right. I have to go or I'll never be able to move past it. What if this is the key to protecting Knova? My gaze returns to my brother. "That's the thing. I'll never get over my past until I face them. If I turn back, it will always haunt me. It's time for my cowardice to end." As I speak the words, the more truth I find in them. "I'll be honest, I'm not thrilled about going back, but I need to. It's time for retribution."

Owen smirks. *I like the idea of that.*

The tent beside us unzips, and Mer walks out. She has a huge grin. "Did I just hear it's time to cause some hell?"

She's right. It's time to right some wrongs of my past.

Scowling, Logan crosses his arms. "No, it's not time to cause hell. Do you not remember anything? It's best to play your part and be invisible. I expect something like this from them, but not you. What in Knova is going on with you?"

He doesn't get it. But to be honest, I couldn't see what was going on while I lived there. When it's all you've ever known, it becomes a matter of survival. "We never were invisible. Do you really think that? Don't be so naïve, Logan. We've always had a target on our backs. Elizabeth lashed out at us when she could, and we were mere puppets that the king liked to intimidate and play with." Who do they think they are? Do they think they are above the law? "I'm done living in fear of them. I'm done being a target for their tantrums, and they must face the consequences for how they've treated us."

Logan's face turns red and his jaw ticks. "You're safe now. He thinks you're dead. What can you do anyways? At the end, all you ever did was cause problems." He looks at me with disgust. "All you're going to do is cause problems again and get all of us hurt. You're weak. Don't let them fool you into thinking you're strong."

Hurt radiates from my very core. This is what my brother thinks of me? He thinks I'm a troublemaker and a weakling? Who the hell does he think he is?

Before I can even blink, Owen grabs Logan by the shirt, anger clear on his face. "Do not ever talk to her that way again. She's stronger than you'll ever be. Don't ever try to undermine her confidence." He pushes Logan.

My brother stumbles back a few steps, surprise clear on his face.

Owen growls. "She may be your sister and that's why you're acting out. I think, in some twisted way, you're trying to protect her, but stop. I will not tolerate it."

The young guard runs over and glances around warily. "Sir, are you okay?"

Logan straightens and nods.

Walking out of the tent next to us, Willow stands next to my brother, patting his back. "Yes, he's okay. There was a misunderstanding, but I think it's all been cleared up." She glances at him, raising an eyebrow. "Hasn't it?"

"Yes, it has." He scratches the back of his head and glances at William. "Let's break down the rest of the tents and load up."

"Yes, sir." The young guard salutes and heads off to follow the command.

I turn, avoiding my brother, and begin breaking down the tent.

Owen is beside me, helping within seconds. *He didn't mean it. Don't let him get to you.*

I bite my lip and take a deep breath. He's right, but it hurts. I don't want to analyze this right now. I've got more important things to worry about, such as breaking down the tent, heading back to Agrolon, and seeing my mother.

Soon, the tents are torn down and we are loading up our items.

I head off to make sure the fire is extinguished and find Jacob and Mer together. "Lover's quarrel?"

He looks at the ground, avoiding my gaze.

Mer spins toward me. "Oh, no. We were just discussing something."

I giggle. "Like what?"

She hesitates, which is unlike her.

Jacob nudges her arm. "Go ahead. She's one of us."

What in Knova does that mean? "What the hell is going on?"

She glances around, taking in the surroundings.

Then, they both walk closer to me.

She narrows her eyes. "Why didn't you tell me that your brother has powers, too? I thought we were sisters."

I take a step back, shaking my head. She must be mistaken. "He doesn't. What are you talking about?"

Jacob sighs. "So, you don't know?"

Are they crazy? I throw my hands up in the air. "He doesn't have powers. I would know."

She lets out a breath and grimaces. "Sorry, I didn't mean to accuse you, but he does. You know I can read things like this. His power is weak, but it's there."

That can't be right. There has to be an explanation for this. A rustling noise comes from the main campsite, so I place my finger to my lips. This is something we don't want getting out to everyone else at this point.

Owen steps out and smirks. "You guys are acting guilty of something." He points at Mer. "What did you do?" He walks over to me and pulls me next to him.

I glance up at him, inhaling his scent and nestling closer. "She said my brother has power."

He stiffens and glances at his sister. "Are you sure?"

My heart fills with love. He didn't accuse me of withholding information. The thought didn't even enter his mind.

Mer sighs. "What is up with you and Ari doubting me? Yes, I'm sure. Like I told her, it's weak but there."

I bite my bottom lip. I haven't told them this before, so I'm not sure how they are going to take the news. "My brother and I have a bond of sorts. He can sense my feelings if I let him, and I his. Could it be because of our connection?"

Owen looks at me. "Why haven't you told us this before?"

I shrug. "Because it never came up or crossed my mind. I hadn't thought about it since I came to Noslon. I thought I would never see my brother again."

He nods. "All right, well, we will have to figure this out later. The Agrolon guards are getting anxious, and we need to be heading out. They have been out here for three months and are anxious to get home."

What? They've been out here that long? I'd be ready to get home, too. "All right, let's go. Let's not mention anything to my brother right now. The guards are already suspicious of the way he's acting."

Jacob nods, and we head toward the others. The site is packed up and the guards are waiting on us on their horses.

Willow is leaning against the carriage, a smirk on her face. "Glad you all could make it."

We begin crowding into the carriage when Ares appears. Thank goodness. I would rather ride on him instead of in that cramped space with Mer whining the whole time. I walk over to him and pet his side. "Hey, boy, I'm sure glad you came."

"Ari... get over here," Mer calls from in the carriage.

Owen grabs my hand.

Oh, no. That's not happening. I shake my head. "I can't ride with her. There is no way. I'm riding Ares."

He grins. "Why'd you think I was heading over here to you? I want to ride with you. I enjoyed the ride yesterday."

Even after all this time, when he flirts with me, it steals my breath away.

He pulls me toward him and kisses my lips.

Before things can get too involved, Ares nudges my back, making me fall into Owen.

I laugh. Did a horse just interrupt us?

Owen grumbles, "Even the horse gives us a hard time when we kiss."

I turn back toward the stallion and pet him. "Mind if we ride?"

He stomps like always and allows me on his back.

Owen follows, sitting behind me.

As soon as we are settled, Ares trots up to the Agrolon guards.

My brother cuts his eyes over at me. "Are you guys ready?"

I nod my head, trying to act confident. I've got this. We all take off then, heading through the woods.

‡

WHEN THE WOODS BEGIN THINNING, I KNOW WE ARE CLOSE to Agrolon. My body tenses, and my heart speeds up. Am I making the wrong decision? Should I turn back? What is the king going to say when he sees me?

Owen encircles my waist with his arms, pulling me flush against him. *I can hear your thoughts, because they are so frantic. We've got this. I know I was concerned at first, but you are the strongest, most loving, and kickass woman I know. If you weren't, there is no way you'd ever be my other half.*

Here is hoping he's right. I nestle into his chest. *I love you, Owen.*

He pecks the top of my head, squeezing me. *I love you, too. Forever and always.*

After a little longer, the old Pearson house comes into view.

I haven't seen it since that last night of practicing.

Logan glances back at me, trying to catch my attention.

I'm still not over his words from earlier, so I ignore him. *Owen, this is where I trained with Lydia.*

Ares trots over, moving close to the house. It had always looked worn but well-kept before, but today, I notice that it appears to be in excellent condition. Does someone live here now? I motion for the horse to go closer so we're right next to the house.

Leaning forward, Owen gazes in the window.

"Oh, don't be alarmed." William comes up next to us. "No one lives here. That's why it's in such horrible condition. It's been deserted for some time."

He grins at me and trots off back over toward the other guards.

I glance behind me. "Am I crazy or does it look like it's in good condition?"

"I agree with you. That's strange." Owen glances at his mother. "We need to talk to Mother as soon as possible."

I nod, but Ares doesn't want to leave. I lean down. "We need to follow them. That one guard is my brother, and he's taking me to see the rest of my family."

The stallion snorts but leaves.

Much to my chagrin, it's hard for me to leave this house, too, but we have things to do. We continue on our way, and I realize that the closer we get, the sicker the trees look and the drier the grass is.

Soon, Claire's parents' house comes into view. Memories of our time together flash through my mind. Oh goodness, how I've missed her.

We walk past the house, but I don't see Grace or Derek anywhere in sight.

Our pace is quick, and soon, we make it to town.

It looks even less vibrant here.

Everyone is bustling with chores, but the food they are selling at the market doesn't look as fresh as it used to.

Way too soon, we are making our way between the village and the palace.

Owen moves his hands from my waist and rubs my shoulders. "I've got you and will always protect you. Even when you don't need me to, I've got you covered."

Why am I being such a coward? Am I going to let my demons intimidate me? The palace comes into view, and my heart races. Maybe this is a terrible decision; however, it's really too late to change my mind now.

The guards speed up, desperate to get home.

All too soon, we reach the palace gates and are being herded inside. We head over to the stables and unload our things.

Logan makes his way to me, letting out a deep breath. "I sure hope you all know what you're doing."

I open my mouth to respond, but someone takes a sharp intake of air and squeals. I turn toward the noise.

Claire is standing there, her mouth wide open. "Is it really you?" She bypasses my brother and has me in her arms. "I can't believe it. You're here and alive. My goodness, I've missed you." She buries herself against me in a tight hug.

Owen comes over and watches the whole scene.

Logan waits a minute but soon walks over to where we're standing. "Baby, you need to get back to our quarters."

Standing up straight, she points her finger at him.

"No... No, I'm not going anywhere. That's what got us in the mess to begin with. I'm not leaving her side."

Another guard has made it here, and he looks over at my brother. "King Percy is requesting the Noslon King in the throne room."

He nods. "Yes, sir. We will be there right away."

The guard nods and heads off, leaving us all alone for a few more minutes.

Mer comes out of the stables and heads straight over to me. "When do we get to dress up?"

Of course, that would be her priority. She's very similar to Claire in that regard. "Soon enough, we'll be stuck in those dreadful dresses." I cringe at the thought.

Claire's smile spreads across her face. "Some things never change."

My brother is not even paying attention to what's going on. He glares at Owen. "Come on. We need to get going. We don't want to make the king mad."

Taking his place beside me, Owen takes my hand.

Placing her hand to her chest, Claire's face is almost comical.

Logan grabs her hand, leading the way.

Jacob walks up on the other side of me, and Willow and Mer walk behind us.

I almost laugh. They have me surrounded, protecting me. This is what family is supposed to be about.

We enter into the palace, and it seems so wide and empty.

Leading the way, my brother walks up the long, white stone stairway, which leads into the throne room. He glances back one last time before he enters.

"Finally. It's about damn time you idiots returned. You better have found the Noslon King." King Percy's loud voice echoes against the walls.

We walk in behind Logan, and the room is silent.

I take a deep breath and glance around. King Percy is there, of course, along with Nick, Sam, and King Michael.

Nick's eyes are wide as he stares at me.

Sam's mouth drops open.

King Percy's face turns blood red. His neck is splotchy with restrained rage.

The one person who is composed in the whole situation is King Michael.

Taking a step toward me, Nick trembles and his tone is soft. "Is that really you?"

I bite my tongue, preventing my laugh from escaping. Yes, it's me. You're not seeing a ghost.

Owen tugs me toward him, his arm slipping around my waist. He moves me forward with him. "I am the King of Noslon."

Nick stops in his tracks, his face stark white.

Pulling Sam over next to him, King Michael is calm and collected.

However, Sam is glaring at Owen's arm that is touching me.

King Percy steps forward. "Is this some kind of joke? Do you take me for a fool?"

Smirking, Owen removes his hand from my waist, taking my hand in his. "Well, if you think this is a joke, then maybe you are."

I bite my lip, trying not to laugh. It's kind of funny, though.

King Percy is an older version of Nick, with blonde hair and blue eyes. However, he's not as tall as I remember him being. It always seemed like he was twice my size, but he's not even a head taller than me. He's not all that muscular, either. The fear that used to control me is no longer present. He's just a man desperate for power and control, and I used to give him exactly that.

He glares at our joined hands then gazes at me. "Well, thank goodness you aren't dead. We all thought you went crazy and killed yourself when you realized there was no chance for you and Prince Nicholas." He puts his hands over his heart and motions toward my and Owen's joined hands. "Luckily, you just ran away with a broken heart and aligned yourself with the self-proclaimed 'King of Noslon'."

I smirk. "Yes, that's what I did. I ran away from everything I have ever known due to a broken heart."

My brother hisses at me. "Ari…"

Willow walks out from the back of the room where she had been hidden. "Oh… King Percy. So nice to see you again."

Jerking back, King Percy looks at her, and his face loses a bit of color. "Queen Willow?"

King Michael's face also pales at Willow's presence. He looks at King Percy. "How did you not know about this?"

Snorting, Mer's tone is soft but loud. "Because we didn't want you to know."

The Agrolon King looks at Owen and then back at his mother. "Is this true? This boy is truly the King of Noslon?"

A snide smile crosses her face, and she nods. "Yes,

unfortunately, King Alban passed a while back. Our son has been leading the people of Noslon for a while."

King Percy's head tips back a little. "How did I not know this?"

Does he think we are all idiots? Everyone is aware of his motivations; he's just too self-righteous to realize it.

Owen barks out a chuckle. "Because it's not any of your business and doesn't affect you. It's not like we have been allies."

King Percy's head snaps in our direction again, his jaw clenched. "It would have been nice to know, just the same."

Keeping his composure, Owen shrugs. "I'm sure it would have been."

The Agrolon King huffs and moves closer to us.

I'm about to take a step back.

Owen's voice enters my head. *Do not take a step back. Remember, you are my queen.*

Okay, so maybe some of my old ways are present. I take a deep breath and hold my ground, but the orange scent of this vile king infiltrates my nose. Flashbacks to my beatings push to the forefront of my mind.

Owen stiffens and his breaths become shallow. He squeezes my hand. *That will not happen to you again. I won't allow it.*

I'm slammed back into the present. Oh, crap, he saw flashes of my memories. You'd think I'd be better with this whole bond thing after a year. However, if I didn't know him so well, I wouldn't notice any changes in his demeanor. His face is his standard blank mask, but I can feel the anger pouring off him.

"I would have liked to say my goodbyes to your father. Even though we weren't close, he was another ruler which deserved respect." King Percy looks up at the ceiling.

If that isn't a sign of a lie, I don't know what else is.

Scowling, Owen's shoulders tense. "I'm sure that's why you would have come to visit."

The king raises his chin. "Are you insinuating something?"

Owen smirks. "I'm not insinuating anything. Anyways, we are here, as you requested. Can you please inform us of what's going on with Crealon?"

I swear, the Agrolon king is about to lose it. He's not used to being treated this way. Everyone else just follows his command without question, so Owen's attitude has him thrown off-kilter.

He clears his throat and puffs up his chest. "Yes, apparently, as we have suspected, they have started rallying. Even though Emerson is our future Queen, they have come to the conclusion she is not the Savior and that we are overconfident and weak. They plan on taking us all down and ruling us with a lead fist. I will not have that. I will rule over Knova." His voice echoes against the room's walls.

It's a vast room made for an egotistical king. It's been a year, but the same stark white walls stand, along with the thrones being centered and up on a pedestal. The one thing that is different is another set of throne chairs to the left and right of the main ones, which are lower and smaller in size. I guess it's for Owen and King Michael.

Silence extends until my brother speaks up. "My dear

king, my mother would appreciate a visit from my sister. It's been a tough year for all of us."

King Percy sighs and nods. "Of course. Please, take her to your mother. I'd like to talk to King Owen alone." He motions for Logan to go.

I stiffen.

Go on, princess. My mate squeezes my hand. *I think it's for the best. I will find you within the hour, promise.*

I sigh, relenting. I do want to see my mother. I turn and walk toward Claire and Logan and can feel Nick and Sam staring at me.

Mer steps in front of me and winks. "We won't be long."

They better not be or I will find my way back here.

We walk out of the room, making our way toward my old quarters.

When I'm a safe way from the throne room, I stop. "What the hell?"

My brother jerks around. "You mean thank you?"

Claire tilts her head to the side.

I put my hands on my hips. "No, I should have stayed with Owen. That's where I need to be. The reason I didn't throw a fit is because I do want to see Mother."

He takes a deep breath and throws his hands up. "The king was focused on you. We had to get away."

Claire reaches out and touches his shoulder.

I bite my lip. "So what if he was watching me?"

He steps toward me. "Do you not remember what used to happen? Do you want him to pay attention to you? Do you think *Owen* can protect you?"

Did he just say that? I take a step toward him and push

my finger into his chest, glaring. "I don't need anyone to protect me. I can take care of my own damn self."

He grabs my hand, shoving it away. "You're just the Savior's sister. You're nothing. Don't think you're more important or powerful than you are."

"Okay... that's enough." Claire tugs him back and out of my face. "Look, you both are being irrational and mean to each other."

Maybe that's true, but I can't stand being spoken down to. I'm not tolerating it any longer.

"You...," she points at me, "be nice. Your brother has been beside himself since the day you disappeared or whatever the hell happened. He thought you were dead. I know you didn't leave on purpose, but your disappearance left a hole behind in a lot of people's hearts. It affected all of us."

Wow... okay. I guess I hadn't thought of it that way. How would I feel if I ran into my brother after I thought he had been dead for a year?

She then turns to my brother and points a finger at him. "And you... stop being overprotective. You're being a jerk and trying to get her to act like the old Ari. She's hardened, and that's okay. Don't try to make her lose confidence in herself. She's the same person, just a little wiser and maybe...," she smirks, "badass."

He scowls at her. "Do not encourage her. She's been away for over a year. I think she's forgotten what it's like. We must stay under the radar to survive." His attention lands back on me. "You come in here with the King of Noslon. What are you thinking?"

I cross my arms. "I remember perfectly what it was

like living under his rule, but you have no idea what I've endured or what I am capable of at this point. As for Owen, I'm thinking he's my other half, and where he goes, I go."

"Yes, right into the lion's den. Do you think this is going to go over well? He's taking advantage of you, despite whatever you think is going on between you all." He waves his hand back and forth. "I bet you he'll side with King Percy as soon as their conversation is over. He used you to get to them."

Who the hell does he think he is? My power churns inside me, and I raise my hand in front of my chest, pushing it toward him so that he is against the palace wall. I don't push him hard, but I have to make a point. This ends now.

His eyes widen and his mouth drops open a little.

Claire gasps. "Ari…"

I ignore her and glower at my brother. "You've said your piece, but at this point, you are disrespecting me. I'm done listening, and we will not talk about this anymore." I take a step toward him, making sure he meets my gaze. "You have no right talking about my relationship with anyone. You haven't been around, nor do you know what I've endured this past year. Now, please, take me to my mother." I release the power that was holding him in place.

He stares at me for a moment, at a loss.

Claire stands beside me and reaches out to take my hand. "Come on, drama queen. Let's go." She pulls me back on course.

My brother follows behind, not saying a word.

She looks at me and smiles. "I've missed you so much. I can't believe you're back."

Fighting off the tears, I blink. "I've missed you, too. You have no idea."

Before long, we walk up to my old home. It's funny, because it doesn't feel like it's mine in any way now. My home is with my mate, and there is no coming back to this.

She opens the door to my old quarters.

Mother's voice comes from her bedroom. "I heard some guards have returned. I think Logan may be back home. How long has it been since...?" She cuts off when she walks into the den and sees me. She stops in her tracks, her eyes widening, and clutches her chest. Shaking her head, tears moisten her eyes. "Is it really you?"

A tear slides down her cheek. After just a moment, she rushes toward me, collecting me in her arms. "How is this possible? The king said you threw yourself over the balcony after not being able to take Prince Nicholas' rejection."

I return her embrace, tears falling down my face. "I didn't, but it's a detailed story. I'm here."

She clutches me closer.

I have missed her so much, much more than I realized after all the time that has passed.

After a while, she loosens her hold and looks at my face. "Oh, I've wished for this moment. I knew you couldn't be dead. You have too much to live for. Where have you been? You're stronger than before you left."

I'm about to answer my mother when there is a loud knock at my door.

Mother glances up. "Who could that be?"

Before anyone can respond, the door bursts open, and Owen comes walking in, followed by Jacob, his mother, and Mer.

My mother gasps.

But my mate is focused on me. "I may kill him."

Mer walks up beside him and takes in the scene, but of course, she has no filter. "Nope, it's happening. Just a matter of when. I hope I'm able to help." She flips her hair and glances my way. "He hates you."

She acts as if this is brand new information. Not to me. I'm aware of his hatred and, at one time, wore constant and painful reminders.

Being this close to my mate and not distracted by my familial drama, I can feel the tension and anger pouring off of him. The only other time he's been this upset was when Rose tried to kill me.

I step toward him. "What happened?"

He takes a deep breath. "Did you know that, if I were willing to terminate any type of relationship with you, I could be married to Princess Elizabeth. They are throwing a ball in my honor, and we could be wed during the event."

Of course, let's strip any amount of happiness from my life.

My mother gasps. "How is that possible? She's engaged to Prince Samuel."

My brother decides to speak up. "So, is this your way of saying that you're moving on?"

Red, hot anger fuels both Owen and me.

Before I realize what's happening, Owen grabs my brother by his shirt and shoves him against the wall.

Logan bucks but doesn't move an inch.

Getting in his face, Owen growls out, "I get that you don't like me. I'm not a fan of you, either. I know you love your sister and spent your life trying to protect her." He tilts his head in my direction. "But you don't feel as if you know her, and you're acting out, wanting her to revert to her old ways. It's not going to happen. She is not the same person she was when you last saw her. I'm not leaving, and she won't leave me. So, it'll be easier if you just accept the circumstances. She is my mate, and there is no changing that."

Mer grabs my hands and tugs me over to plop down on the couch. She covers her mouth but speaks loudly. "I bet some chocolate on my brother."

Smirking, Willow comes to sit on the other side of me and pats my leg. "Don't worry. This is where they start accepting each other. They both have to realize that each one has your best interest at heart and show that they are willing to fight for you."

Claire and Mother are in the doorway with wide eyes, watching the whole interchange.

I sigh, giving up on any sense of normalcy, and look at the door. "Jacob, I believe you are the only one with manners. Please, come on in and make yourself at home." I point around the den and kitchen area then smirk. "Just, please, try not to say too much. We all know how you are."

Mer snorts. "Yes, please, save us from all your opinions."

Ignoring us, Jacob walks into the room and heads to Owen. "Need me to take over?"

Owen and Logan are staring at each other. Owen shoves him once more before letting him go. "Nah, we're good."

Making his way to the couch, Owen scowls at Mer. "Move, now."

She sticks her tongue out but gets up.

He sits beside me and pulls me to his side, wrapping his arms around me. He leans toward me and breathes me in.

My mother must have had some sense returned to her. "Um... hello. I'm Jo, Ariah's mother."

Willow smiles at her and rises. "I'm so sorry for the intrusion. My son needed to get to Ariah. I'm Willow, Owen's mother, and this," she points at Mer, "is my daughter, Meredith. The gentleman over in the corner is Jacob. He's a close family friend."

My mother smiles in return. "Okay, so why in Knova would King Percy offer Princess Elizabeth as a wife? I just don't understand. She's engaged to the Prince of Orlon."

Willow glances back at us. "Well, because my son is the King of Noslon."

My mother's face loses its color. "Wait..." She looks at me. "You're being courted by the King of Noslon?"

Mer cracks up.

Owen leans toward me, his arms stiffening around my waist. "It's more than just courting. This is ridiculous."

I smirk. *Let's not throw too much on my mother at one time, okay?*

Answering for me, Willow smiles. "Yes, she sure is."

When my mother glances at me, disappointment is clear on her face.

Claire clears her throat. "Well, I'm Claire, Ariah's sister and Logan's wife. Are you guys hungry? It is lunch time."

I smile at her declaration. I love hearing her call me her sister, but it hurts at the same time. I missed their wedding. There are some memories I just won't get to share with them. And what the hell is King Percy doing trying to marry Elizabeth off to Owen?

Owen chuckles. *She won't touch me, don't worry. I'm all yours.* I glance back at him and smile. *But, princess, we need to talk when we are alone.*

I hate when he does this. I want to know what it is and don't want to wait. *Why didn't you just wait if you aren't willing to discuss right now?*

He pecks my lips, chuckling.

Logan grunts and channels his displeasure into me.

I ignore him. Since running into him in the forest, he hasn't been happy with any of my actions or decisions.

Mer pulls me up from the couch. "Okay, let's go eat. I'm hungry. Lead the way."

I look over at Mother. "What do we have to eat?"

Standing, Owen takes my hand. "You all don't eat together?"

My brother leans against the wall with his arms crossed. "Yes, the palace residents can eat in the dining hall, but we choose to eat at our homes to stay out of the king's way."

Owen tugs me toward the door. "Then we will eat with them."

"No…" My brother pushes off from the wall and heads to the kitchen. "We can find something here."

Owen sighs and turns to face my brother. "Look… I'm the King of Noslon. I can't cower down to King Percy. It'll make us look weak."

He pulls on me, but my brother grabs my other hand. "Then go. We can eat just fine without you."

Before this can turn into some testosterone battle, I raise a hand toward each of them. "I don't want to eat in the dining hall either."

Logan relaxes at my statement.

Owen tenses but waits for me to continue.

"However, I will be joining Owen." I sigh. "I can't do this anymore. I'm tired of being manipulated and bullied. This ends now."

My brother's breathing becomes erratic, his hands clenched. "You're going to get her killed."

Even though it's untrue, my brother believes that in his core. I don't know how to help him see otherwise.

Claire takes a deep breath, nodding. She watches me for a second but takes a step toward me. "Okay, let's do this. I'm trusting you."

"Wait… what?" Logan grabs her arm. "There is no way in hell."

Claire removes herself from his grasp and crosses her arms. "If she is eating in the dining hall, well, so am I."

She loops her arm through mine and pulls me to the door, opening it.

Owen walks up on the other side, and we start our path to lunch.

Mer, Jacob, and Willow follow right behind us, while Mother and Logan drag slowly in the back.

Leaning into Claire, I smile. "You don't have to do this. I don't want to cause problems between you and my brother."

She glances at Owen and then back to me. "You're not the same. He isn't handling it well." She leans closer. "Something pulses out of you, a strength that has always been there but hidden. I've always known you had it, but he feels like you needed a protector. He can't stand it, but you can't fold. Logan just needs time to come to grips with it. You're my friend. I will always support you, and you need that now just as much as ever."

Thank Knova I have her back. She's positive and loyal, and I'm grateful to have her back on my side.

When we reach the door, Owen steps up and opens it for us. "After you."

I glance at him and take a steadying breath. The games are about to begin. The king started it by offering Elizabeth as Owen's bride. What the Agrolon King doesn't realize is that we've promised ourselves to each other and will be married soon. I can't be weak for him or myself.

His eyes soften as he projects, *I love you.*

I smile and walk past him, holding my head high. Game on.

Chapter Three

As soon as I walk through the doors, the noise in the dining hall stops. The royals are seated at their table, and I'm surprised to find a third royal table on the other side of the Agrolon family.

King Percy stands and walks over to Owen, shaking his hand. He turns and faces the room. "I was wondering when the King of Noslon would grace us with his presence. In fact, I was just about to send someone out to look for him." He spreads his arm out. "So, two miracles have happened. One, we have finally reached King Owen of Noslon, and he is here to help with our fight that is coming against the West. And what do we find in his tow?" He turns to me, his eyes hardening.

I can almost smell the disgust coming off of him, he feels it so strongly.

Looking back toward the other side of the dining hall, he grins. "No other than our runaway, Lady Ariah. She has returned since her heart has had some time away from Prince Nicholas."

He takes in the others standing behind Owen. "King Owen, your Noslon natives may sit with you at your royal table. The others can find seating elsewhere." He turns his back on me, dismissing me.

Taking my hand, Owen's tone is loud. "No, I would like for them all to sit at my table."

Spinning back around, King Percy glares at our joined hands. He takes a few deep breaths. "Of course, as you wish." He heads back to his table but turns around to glare at me one last time before he sits beside Nick.

Leading us to the table, Owen makes sure that I sit on his right side so that both he and I are center, and Willow sits on the other side of him. Mer comes over and sits on my other side, and Jacob sits across from her. My mother sits across from me, with Logan beside her, and Claire on the other side at the end. It feels as if all the attention is on us, and I'm sure my placement next to my mate is noted by all.

Our food is served. It's a meal of lamb and vegetables along with their hearty bread. It is good, but the Noslon food is just as good since they count on fresh kills just like Agrolon. However, they eat deer and gamey type foods, which differs from this kingdom.

Logan and Mother have tension rolling off them. They are looking around, waiting for something to happen.

However, Claire seems more intrigued.

Owen eats with one hand and puts his other one on my inner thigh below the table. We both need the physical connection.

Taking a bite of her food, Mer looks over at Jacob and talks with a mouthful of food. "This is good, but I'm ready for dessert. I sure hope it's chocolate."

Jacob smirks, but as usual, continues eating.

Watching the Agrolon royals, Willow turns back to the table and looks over at Owen and me. "I hope you're both ready for the next few days. It will be challenging, mainly for Ariah, but a lot will come to light."

Owen sighs. "Please, not now. We can discuss this later."

Leaning across the table, my mother stares at Willow. "What do you mean, and how do you know this?"

My mother is very observant. We need to be careful with our words around her. I don't want her to know more than she needs to.

Putting both elbows on the table, Mer places her chin in her hands. "Oh, just ignore her. She always talks like this."

Times like these are when I love her the most. She has a way of downplaying situations.

Snorting, Jacob speaks up for once. "I don't know why you and your brother have to give her such a difficult time. She ends up being right."

Mer cuts her gaze to him. "Hey, why don't you go back to your sullen ways?"

I laugh. We give him a hard time about not speaking, but when he does, one of us tells him to be quiet.

Owen gives me a small smile.

He seems tense tonight, and I'm not sure why. We'll figure it out… together. We always do.

Dessert is served and, much to Mer's delight, it's a

JEN L. GREY

triple chocolate cake. She takes a big bite and moans loudly.

Claire chuckles, her face bright with humor.

My brother watches Mer with a disgusted look across his face. Logan huffs. "You guys do realize this is not a game. My sister's life could be a stake."

Glaring at him, Owen slams his spoon on the table. "See, that's where you're wrong. This is a game and always has been. You have been a pawn all along, and that's one reason why Ariah was at risk in the first place."

Oh, crap. We can't do this here. We are garnering too much attention.

The Agrolon table is watching us. King Percy is smiling. And now, Owen has captured Elizabeth's attention. She's biting her lips, smirking.

I reach under the table and hold my mate's hand. He's about to come unglued with the whole situation. What my brother doesn't realize is that Owen is great at masking his emotions and seeming in control. However, he's the most upset about me being back.

Pure hatred crosses Logan's face. "You've been here for all of a half a day, and you think you know what is going on? You think I haven't protected her?"

This has to stop now. I lean forward. "Stop this. We are making a scene. I don't know what's going on between the two of you, but it has to stop." I turn and look at Owen. "We need to make a scene on our own terms, not let whatever testosterone battle you have going on with my brother take over your good sense."

He squeezes my leg and nods. "You're right. I'm sorry."

Claire raises an eyebrow, taking in the whole exchange.

Taking another large bite, Mer points her spoon at Logan. "You just need to chill out. We know what we are doing."

He opens his mouth.

But Claire puts her hand on his arm. "Just relax. They are right. We can talk later."

The table goes silent, and my mother is shifting in her seat.

After a few minutes, people are finishing their meals, and Elizabeth pops up from her seat. Her eyes land right on Owen, then flicker over to me. All right, so the dragon princess of Agrolon is making her approach.

She saunters up to us. Her dark red hair is pulled up on top of her head with curls cascading down. She has a tight, emerald green dress on, which I find funny since she's wearing Orlon's color and coming over to meet a different man. Her lips are painted dark red.

She snarls when she looks at me. "Well, look who it is. It's as if you came back from the dead." She turns her attention to Owen and purrs. "I'm sorry you've had to take care of her. If it weren't for her sister, she'd be living in that shack outside the village." She lowers her voice some and smirks. "She's not up to our caliber, if you know what I mean."

Elizabeth squeezes between us and tries to put her hand on his chest.

Owen catches her arm and lifts his chin. "You'd behave in this manner with your fiancé sitting less than twenty feet away?"

She licks her lips. "Well, Father said that there might be another arrangement coming to play, and I can't say I'm disappointed. I could take care of you in ways she never could."

I'm about to come unglued. Who the hell does she think she is? "Yeah, you're right about that."

Her head jerks toward me, her eyes wide. "Excuse me?"

Owen stands, followed by Jacob and Mer.

Elizabeth smirks and reaches out for Owen's shoulder. "Don't worry, you'll forget her after tomorrow. I'll make sure of it."

The jerk lets her touch his shoulder. What the hell is he doing? I know he's mine, but this is a game I'm not willing to partake in. However, I'll be damned if I let her know.

My mother watches me, concern outlining her face.

Walking over to me, Logan takes my hand. "Come on. Let's go."

I look Owen in the eye, wondering what his game plan is.

He just stares back at me with his usual indifference. Okay, then. "No, I'm good. I think I'd like to visit with some people before heading back to the quarters. I mean, Elizabeth is right. I haven't been around in a while."

Snarling, Elizabeth steps closer into Owen. "That's Princess Elizabeth to you. You seem to have forgotten your place while you were gone. Do not forget who rules you."

I tilt my head and smile. "I wasn't able to before. Why

would that be any different now?" Someone's hand touches the center of my back, and I turn to find Sam.

He's looking down at me. "Since Princess Elizabeth is giving Owen a tour, how about you keep me company in her absence?"

No, I don't want to. His betrayal springs to mind.

I force myself to smile and nod. If Owen is going to play like this, it's only fair that I return the favor.

Elizabeth glares at Sam, but he ignores her.

I loop my arm through Sam's, and he leads us out of the dining hall. Okay, maybe this wasn't the best idea. I did kind of run away from Owen without any explanation.

We walk in silence, and it won't be long before the one dreaded conversation begins.

After a few moments, I realize he is leading us to the garden, my former favorite place. He leads us to my spot. The garden is wilted and in worse shape than the village grounds. My favorite purple flowers are browning with only a hint of their original color bleeding through.

I walk away from him, toward the big tree that is leaning that I used to lay under. The jasmine has a faint smell, but it's not as sweet as it once was.

"Yeah, as you can tell, the garden is dying." He sighs. "We have no clue why. Prince Nicholas and I are doing everything to keep your memory... I mean, the garden alive."

I flinch. I guess the fun starts here.

He walks up closer behind me. "Why did you run away from me?"

I sigh and turn around. As always, he's dressed in his

royal attire with the trademark emerald green woven throughout. His brown eyes are searching for something in my face. "Sam, you know why I left Orlon."

He licks his lips. "No, I need to know what happened. Why did you run away? Why did you not trust me?"

I chuckle. Why are we doing this? We both know what happened.

His forehead creases, as if he truly doesn't understand how he betrayed me.

"I heard you and your father." I take a step toward him. "You were engaged to Elizabeth and didn't tell me. You gave me an engagement ring when you were already betrothed."

He lifts both hands up. "You know I wouldn't have followed through. I love you, Ari. I would have defied my father and married you."

Is he serious? I can't contain the laughter in me any longer. All my life, I've relied on others to protect me. I trusted people without having them earn that right. Why was I so naïve? Tears are pouring out of my eyes from my laughter. It's taken twenty years, but at least I have a sense of who I am for the first time in my life.

Sam's concern is etched across his entire face. "Are you okay? What have they done to you?"

I take a deep breath, trying to get my emotions all together. "They haven't done anything to me, except help me become who I was always meant to be. You and Agrolon have hurt and betrayed me. No, I don't trust you. You were going to cut me loose. Maybe you would have helped me find a way out, instead of trying to kill me like King Percy, but you would have done what was expected from you. That's not what makes me unable to trust you, though. You were engaged to Elizabeth and proposed to me. You were so focused on claiming me and keeping me from Nick, that you didn't care about what my future would entail. You're just like any other royal in this place. Don't pretend you aren't."

His mouth drops open. "What the hell does that mean? I love you."

I bite my lip. "You love the idea of me. Come on, you've always been able to do what you want. Becoming engaged to Elizabeth was your first royal task if you will. You are having to play the dutiful son, and I represent the exact opposite of that. However, I'm not the same girl I was a year ago, and I'm not confused."

"No. No, that's not true." He pulls me toward him and leans down.

Before I can register what's going on, pure pain pulses through my body. What the hell? My body feels as if fire is raging within me.

"Ari?" Sam is screaming and frantic, but I can't hear him.

I remember this feeling from when I was with him in Oslon before, but it is so much worse this time. I fall to my knees, and he bends down, touching me, which makes the pain flare worse. I jerk away and just lay down on the ground, withering. I don't know how much time has passed, but I feel as if I'm dying. Of course it would be in Agrolon.

Thunderous footsteps are moving my way.

"You need to get to her now." Willow's voice somehow filters into my head.

Sam is touching me, trying to help me, but he's pulled away.

Arms circle around me, and I'm pulled into the chest I know and love. The fire is extinguished and I whimper. Owen tightens his arms around me and kisses my forehead.

There's some shuffling and Jacob's loud, raspy voice. "What did you do?"

That's odd. He never talks. I glance over Owen's shoulder.

Sam is looking around, fear and uncertainty playing across his face. "I didn't do anything."

Pulling back, Owen looks at me with concern. "Are you okay?"

I nod, drained from all the pain.

Owen gets up and helps me to my feet. When I'm solid on my feet, he walks over beside Jacob to glare at Sam. "What did you do?"

Sam looks back at him defiantly. "Like I told him," he points to Jacob, "I didn't hurt her."

Stepping closer, Owen gets in his face. "Did you touch her?"

Sam stands his ground. "What does it matter to you? You were preoccupied with Elizabeth."

Owen rears back and punches him in the stomach. "Do not touch her. Do you understand?"

Clutching his stomach, Sam rolls over into the fetal position.

I rush over to them and look at Owen. "What are you doing?"

Power is coursing out of him. He kicks Sam in the leg. "What did he do?"

I put my hands on his chest. "What are you talking about?"

Pulling me against him, he growls, his power reaching out to mine. "He touched you with romantic intentions. Did he kiss you?"

I shake my head. "No, he didn't. He pulled me to him, but I started burning up before he ever did anything."

Sam gets up, holding his stomach. "What the hell is your problem?" He tries to step toward me. "Are you okay?"

Owen blocks him, his fist clenched.

Jacob pushes him back. "Do not go near her."

I don't want to deal with all this. This whole night has gone from bad to worse. "All right, enough." I meet Sam's gaze. "I think we've hashed everything out. It's time for you to go."

He moves around Jacob, so he can see me but doesn't step closer. He's clutching his stomach and is in obvious pain. "But…"

I hold my hand up. "No, don't. I have nothing else to say to you. It's time for you to go." I focus on Owen. "You and I have some things I want to discuss alone."

Sam doesn't move for a moment, just stares at me.

Jacob takes a step toward him.

He sighs and glances at me one last time before he begins limping away. We all watch him leave in silence.

As soon as he is out of sight, Jacob turns toward us. "Are you both okay?"

Willow walks over to me and places her hand on my arm.

I look at them. "I'm okay. What the hell happened?"

Owen reaches for me, but I dodge his hand. He didn't mean to hurt me tonight, and I know there is a reason for him doing so but being slighted by him burns me up.

He rubs his hands down his face. "Come on."

Willow squeezes my arm and gives me a small smile. "Sam had romantic intentions with you."

What? How does she know that? "What do you mean?"

Letting out a breath, she takes a step back. "When you start the bonding process with your mate, if another person tries to form a romantic bond with you, well, your powers rebel. For those who are lucky enough to have a soulmate, your power is made to harmonize and sync with theirs. If someone tries to break that connection, your power retaliates."

How is that possible? My power was attacking me? "But that doesn't make sense. Granted, tonight, it was more intense, but when I was staying in Orlon, that happened before Owen and I connected."

Owen growls. "Can we not talk about this? I don't want to hear about your romance, however brief, with the Orlon Prince."

Willow ignores him. "Your bond with Owen began the day of the blood oath. When your blood connected, your powers combined. I'm assuming, when you had pain similar to tonight, you were involved with Sam in some sort of romantic situation. Tonight was worse for both of you, because the bond had already begun and is much stronger now."

Wait. What? "What do you mean, worse for both of us?"

Owen steps closer to me. "When our bond is threatened in any capacity, we both feel it. Didn't it seem odd how we all rushed to you?"

I glare at him. "I'm surprised you picked up on it, being preoccupied with Elizabeth."

Jacob snorts out laughter.

Owen lets out a deep sigh. "Look, I'm sorry. But you don't have anything to worry about, unlike me. I leave you alone for just a few minutes, and someone is trying to move in."

What the hell did he just say? I place my hand on my hips. "Like Elizabeth wasn't making moves on you."

Jacob clears his throat and takes a few steps away. "Come on, Willow. Why don't we go check on Mer? We did leave her behind with Ariah's moody brother."

They leave, and I refocus my attention on Owen.

He runs his hand through his hair. "Did you feel any pain before that Orlon Prince made his move?"

I shake my head. "No, I didn't."

He takes my hand. "That's because she's not interested in me. She's not a threat to our bond. She and the Agrolon King are trying to make me their pawn."

I let out a breath and look him directly in the eyes. "I get it, but it hurts. Why did you let it go that far?"

Then, his magnificent smile spreads across his face. "For many reasons, but the main one was to cause a little hell."

He tugs me against him. I relent, needing the closeness.

He looks down at me and cups his hand around my cheek. "How do you feel about moving up our wedding?"

I snort. "You mean back? We aren't going to be done with the war in time. We are supposed to be married in less than a month."

He bends down, brushing my lips with his. When he pulls back, his eyes are filled with love. "No, I mean up. King Percy wants a wedding at the conclusion of the ball. I thought we could let him have one, just with a different bride than he plans on."

My heart speeds up, and I bite my lower lip.

He runs his fingers across my cheek. "Your family can be by your side this way." He lowers his forehead and places it on mine. "I'm sorry, but I let Elizabeth do it just so that King Percy thinks he's winning. I don't want his attention on you, but after tonight with the Orlon Prince, I realize I was doing the same thing your brother has been doing, and you're stronger than that. Let's show them we can't be manipulated, that we will always stand together. I know we're bonded, but let's make it official so there is no question."

I smile but put my fingers under his chin. "If you let her touch you again, I won't be as forgiving. I love you and may be bonded to you, but I will be respected. If not, I'll make it on my own."

He nods and meets my gaze. "I'm sorry. I won't make the same mistake twice. I won't ever risk losing you."

I lower my hand from his chin and take his hand. "Come on, I need to get some rest. My wedding is tomorrow."

Chapter Four

✦✦✦

As soon as we walk back into my family's quarters, I notice Claire and Mother sitting on the couch, and Willow, Mer, and Jacob standing in the middle of the den surrounding Logan.

My brother rushes to me and pulls me away from Owen. "You're done messing with her. You've proven where your loyalties lie tonight, and you need to go. I refuse for her to be hurt."

I laugh. "I can't be hurt much more than what I've endured already, so back off. Owen's just playing a game, but we've come to an understanding tonight." I glance back at him.

He nods his head, but for once, doesn't try to take over.

Hurt is clear across my brother's face, but I just don't have the energy to deal with all this drama. 'Aren't you tired of being a pawn?"

Mother and Claire stand up and walk beside him.

His face is one of disbelief. "Are you serious? This is about survival. Don't let him," he points at Owen, "mess with your head."

Why is he acting so crazy? Even Owen is. I swear, this place is woven all in evil. For once, I'm the one with my head on straight. I sigh and walk over to the vacant couch, just needing to sit down. I glance up at my brother. "He's not messing with my head. I've changed. We thought it was about survival, but it's more than that. The king doesn't care if we survive. He has us around because he enjoys our cowardice. It's a game, just like Owen said at dinner. Can we, as good people, allow a selfish, manipulative man to rise to power? Can we continue to let our people be ignored and treated as nuisances?"

Logan must be speechless, because he's quiet.

Mother tilts her head. "What do you expect us to do? Emerson is the Savior, and the king dictates her every move."

Looking down at the table, I shrug. "I'm not expecting you to do anything, but after the king tried to kill me, and after the Orlon betrayals, I'm not content just hiding in the shadows. Me being complacent could have gotten me killed, so why continue down that road? Yes, Emerson is the Savior, not King Percy. I'm tired of treating him like he's sovereign."

Sitting beside me, Willow smiles. She looks at me with her eyes taking on the ethereal glow. "It's getting close to time. You are becoming what is needed."

Okay, I'm creeped out. I mean, she has always been a puzzle, similar to Lydia and Hazel, but I have no clue what she's talking about. I'm not needed at all.

Claire gasps. "Ari, her eyes glow like yours."

Walking toward me, Owen takes my hand. "Mother, you're scaring people."

Willow closes her eyes and opens them back up, and the normal blue shade has returned.

Mother takes a shallow breath and places her hand over her heart.

I'm just so tired. The whole thing with Sam took a lot out of me. I glance over to Mer and Jacob and am surprised to find him holding her hand.

As soon as he notices, he drops it.

Maybe he's finally making his move. It's about time. I look at her. "I need you to find me the perfect dress for the ball. It needs to be gorgeous and all things Noslon."

Her face lights with a huge smile. "I've got you covered."

"Hey," Claire pipes up. "I want in. Pretty dresses are my thing, too."

Mer glares at Claire.

I giggle, because they are similar in this regard. I glance at Mer. "She is an expert, too, so let her help."

I put my hands together. "Sorry, you've just never been to Noslon. I need a dress that represents them, which is why I initially asked only Mer." Laying my head back on the couch, I find Owen. "I'm going to bed. I'm exhausted."

He stands, taking my hand.

My mother steps between us. "Oh, no. No, you don't. I don't care what's happened in the past year, but this is my house." She points to me. "You go to your room. We'll figure out some place for him to sleep."

This is such a maternal reaction that I burst out laughing. I've missed her so much.

Anger flashes across Owen's face.

I glare at him and hug my mother. "Yes, I understand."

His mouth drops open. "Are you serious?"

Mer cracks up laughing.

I just ignore her. "Yes, she's right. This is her home, and you aren't the king here."

Mer comes over and loops her arm through her brother's. "Don't worry. When you guys left me behind at the dining hall, the king came over and told me where our quarters are." She waggles her eyebrows. "It's in the royal wing."

He disentangles himself. "Nope, not happening. I'm not leaving her. You guys can go on. I'll sleep on the couch."

Thank goodness. I didn't want him to leave, but at the same time, it's nice to have my mother taking care of me.

Willow and Jacob head toward the door.

Mer giggles and claps her hands. "I'll start looking through the dresses tonight." She looks at Claire. "I'll bring them over in the morning, and we can pick the final one together. Does that work?"

Claire nods. "I can't wait."

The three of them head out.

When the door shuts, silence descends. I lean over and peck Owen on the lips. "Goodnight."

He grabs my hands and pouts. "You were serious?"

My mother removes his hand from mine. "Yes, she was being serious. One thing that doesn't change is my girl being a nice, caring girl. So, I'll go grab you some sheets for the couch."

Owen stands there, speechless.

Logan is finally smiling.

Claire snorts and grabs my hand. "Come on, let's head to your room for a little while."

I smile at her and we head toward my room. Right before I close the door, I glance back. Owen is watching me but standing in the same spot.

Mother comes in and puts the blankets in his arm. "There you go. Let me know if you need something, and no sneaking in to her room. I'll be getting up to check on you."

I laugh and shut the door. When I turn, I find Claire already sitting on my bed watching me.

She grins. "You look good."

I snort and come over to fall back on the bed. It hasn't changed at all in my absence. "Thanks, I guess. How have you been?" I turn onto my side to face her.

She lays on her side as well. "Well, it's been okay. After you left, Logan and your mother went crazy. We wed immediately, because he was afraid to let me cut of his sight. Then, the king sent him away to search for... well, Owen. So, I haven't seen him a lot. That's one reason why we are living in the same quarters with your mother. I've just been staying in his room."

So, my leaving didn't help them at all. I was determined to stay away for them to have a good life together, and all the king did was rip Logan away from what was left of his family. I'm so tired of being pushed around, and soon, that will all end. Owen and I will unite, and we won't back down, not even to Emerson.

I reach out and place my hand on her arm. "I'm so sorry. I didn't mean for any of this to happen."

She places her free hand on top of mine. "Stop it. You have nothing to be blamed for. When we first met, I didn't understand how much this whole prophecy ran your life. But it came to light after the royal wedding, and it's not your fault. You are just a victim."

I look at the beige bedding and run my hand over it. She's not right. "No, being a victim means you don't have a choice. Maybe I didn't before, but in the past year, I've learned what's right." I glance up. "I won't be the victim any longer."

She sits back up on the bed. "I know, and Owen is good for you. I'm glad you found him."

I smirk. "Me, too. I'd go through all that hell again just to find him."

She takes a deep breath. "I get it. You look exhausted. I'm so glad you're back, but we can catch up later. We have a ball to get ready for."

I groan and flop back on my pillow. "Go see my brother and let me get some rest. You and Mer are both going to attack me first thing in the morning."

She laughs as she shuts the door, and just like that, the void in my heart shrinks. Somehow, I know tomorrow will change everything.

I WAKE TO THE SOUND OF BICKERING. OH, MY GOODNESS,

Owen and Logan are worse than two women. I kick the covers off me and open the door. They are standing beside the kitchen table, and my mother is in between the two of them. "Ugh, guys. Stop. This has to end sometime soon," I mumble, walking past them. I go straight for a large cup and pour some coffee.

Mother laughs. "I see some things don't change."

I raise the cup in her direction. "This is sweet nectar that is needed each morning."

Owen chuckles, startling my mother.

Walking over, I kiss him on the lips. "Yes, he does have a sense of humor. It just takes being around him for a while before you see it."

He pulls back and taps his finger on my nose. "Only you can bring it out."

I tilt my head to the side and wink. "Better be."

Making my way to the table, I sit, taking another sip from my cup.

Owen grabs some muffins off the counter and joins me, putting one in front of me.

After pouring a cup of coffee for herself, my mother joins us at the table.

Logan grabs a muffin and heads to the door. "I'll see you all later. I've got to go fill out a report with the Captain."

I jump up and run to give him a big hug.

He returns the gesture. "You okay?"

I snicker. "Yes, I just missed you is all. I do love you and am glad to be able to see you."

He pats my head and squeezes me tightly. "Love you, too." He turns and leaves.

I make my way back to the table and settle back in, and we all eat our breakfast in silence.

After a little while, my mother clears her throat. "So… last night with Elizabeth must have been the game you were speaking of, even if it was misguided. However, I need to know your intentions with my daughter."

I bite my lip, trying to hold in my laughter.

Owen glances up; annoyance is clear on his face.

It's amusing that he isn't used to being challenged. *Be nice. She is my mother.*

He glances at me and takes my hand, resting it on the table. "You're right. Last night was misguided, but believe me, she put me in my place."

She smiles. "Good. That's what I want to hear."

There is a loud knock on my door, followed by another loud bang. Mer's loud voice infiltrates the room. "Dang it, open this door now."

Owen rolls his eyes and keeps eating.

Jumping up, Mother rushes to the door. "Oh my goodness, there must be something wrong."

Yeah, she doesn't know Mer. If she did, she wouldn't be concerned at all. She opens the door.

Mer is dressed in her standard black, and her hands are empty. She walks in and turns behind her. "Hurry up."

Jacob follows behind, loaded down with dresses and luggage.

My mother hurries to help him. "Oh, how far did you walk like this?"

If I were a betting woman, I'd say he walked like this the whole way.

Mer just comes over and plops down at the table with us. "You guys weren't going to open the door?"

Owen nods. "We were, but after you asked in a civilized manner. We don't jump at your commands."

I look over, and Mother and Jacob are carrying the formal dresses into my room. "Why didn't you help him carry anything?"

She grabs the rest of Owen's muffin off his plate and pops it in her mouth. "He said, 'Oh, let me help.' So... I let him."

Yeah, she's a considerate one. "He said help, not do it all."

She shrugs and reaches over to grab my coffee.

I grab my cup and pull it back. "Boundaries. How many times do we have to go through this?"

She points her finger at me. "Hey, you didn't tell me how delicious the chocolate is here. That's criminal. I'm upset over this. I had to eat your cake last night just to mend my broken heart."

I cut my eyes to Owen. "Is that why she wasn't with you all at the gardens last night?"

He places his fingers on his forehead. "Don't get me started. When we were leaving, she was over at the next table trying to talk them into giving her their dessert as well. And... it had already been eaten off of."

Mer lifts her hands. "I could have cut off the eaten part. It's fine."

I have nothing to say to that. I am speechless and grossed out. "Uh..."

She's shaking her head back and forth. "No... you don't understand. It takes a lot to be this delightful. I need the energy. Who else is going to keep everyone grounded?"

I glance at Owen.

He just shrugs. "Princess, I don't know what to tell you. She's always been like this. I don't understand either."

Mother and Jacob walk back in the room.

She glances at Mer. "Could you not help this kind boy out? Those dresses are heavy."

Mer places her hand on her chest. "He was complaining this morning about not working out the past several days and eating all that food and chocolate last night. I felt it was my duty to help him get his much-needed workout this morning. It was for his wellbeing."

My mother just stares, at a loss for words.

I stand then down the remainder of my coffee. "All right, where is Claire?"

She glances over at me but looks confused. "Oh, she ran out this morning saying she needed to run to her parents' house for a minute. She should be back any second."

I walk through the den and into my room. Covering the bed are at least ten dresses piled up.

Mother enters the room and shuts the door.

What is she doing?

She looks at me and bites her bottom lip. "Are you sure you know what you're doing?"

I huff out a breath and smirk. "Yes, I know what I'm doing."

Her eyes land on the pile of dresses on my bed. "Well… those dresses all kind of look like they could be wedding dresses… so, I guess, I want to know if they are."

My mother has always been so perceptive, and I don't want to disappoint her. I'm not sure how she's going to take my answer, but Owen is it for me. Even if she can't accept it, that won't change. "Yes, they are."

She huffs out a short laugh. "I just got you back." She walks toward me, touching my cheek. "I can't lose you again."

I narrow my eyes. "What do you mean?"

"Do you think the king will allow you to marry Owen? He has his sights on Elizabeth to be wed to him."

I step out of my mother's reach. "Look, I know you are trying to protect me, but Owen is mine."

She sighs and nods. "No, I believe you. It's just, what will the king do to retaliate?"

I throw my hands up in the air. "Who cares? I'm tired of living in fear."

She reaches for my hand, but I back away again, running into the wall.

Her shaking hand reaches for me. "Living in fear is what's kept us safe."

I walk past her, toward the door. "No, that's what got me thrown over the balcony."

Her jaw drops, but I don't stop, slamming the door on my way out of the room.

Standing by my door, Owen pulls me into his arms. "Are you okay?"

I nod but bury my head in his chest.

A loud knock at the door echoes through the room, and Jacob moves to open it.

The older guard from yesterday appears, and his gaze lands on my mate. "King Owen, your presence is requested by King Percy and King Michael. They would like the opportunity to inform you on what the West is doing and discuss a course of action."

Owen glances at me, not wanting to leave.

I force a smile. *Yes, go. I need some time. I'll meet you for lunch.*

His forehead creases. *Are you sure?*

I nod and brush my lips across his cheek.

He sighs and heads toward the guard. "That's fine, but Jacob will accompany me."

The guard opens his mouth, but Owen and Jacob ignore him, walking right past him. The guard turns and rushes after them.

I'm out the door before it can slam. On instinct, I return to the garden and make my way to my favorite spot. Well, at least, it once was. I chuckle, remembering I always made sure I had a blanket, and instead just lie down on the floor to feel the earth under me. This garden is a deeper brown since my last visit. The tree limbs are sagging, and the grass is brown. What happened to this place?

I'm about to revive my little section when there is a rustling close by. I sit up and cringe when Nick comes into view.

He stops when he spots me, and we just stay silent for a few seconds. His blonde hair is styled with his crown on top. He's wearing Agrolon's standard yellow color, and his blue eyes appear haunted. He takes a few steps toward me.

I rise to my feet, wanting to escape.

Falling to his knees before me, he looks up. "I'm so sorry."

I just stare and stay silent. I have nothing to say to him. Yes, I understand that his father had beat him, but that doesn't change the fact that he was a coward. He took me out on the balcony, leading me to my near death, because he was trying to hide from his father.

He steps closer.

And I take a step back. I'm not stepping back out of fear but revulsion. He could have stood up to his father. He could have made a difference for my family... for the village, but he didn't. He stood by while his father advanced with greed and cruelty. "Please, I'm sorry. I still love you."

At those words, I look at his left hand and see the wedding band. I laugh until tears are falling down my face. Does he think this will work this time?

Nick takes a step back and bites his lip.

I take a deep breath, trying to contain myself. "Don't say that again. If you loved me, we would be together and you know it. You are a coward, and you are married to my sister. You need to focus on making her happy and forget about me."

His shoulders sag at those words, and he stares at the ground. "Do you know what it's been like to live with thinking you were dead?"

Is he being serious? I step closer to him, rage boiling. "Look me in the eye."

His head jerks up, and I swear, fear flashes in his eyes. His mouth partially drops open.

I push my finger into his chest. "You don't get pity. You weren't ripped from your family and home. You stayed and married my sister, whom you claim not to love, because your father commanded it. I missed out on my brother's wedding to my best friend. I lost a year of my life with my family. You are not forgiven." I drop my hand and scowl at him.

He fidgets and looks around as if he's trying to escape.

I let out a short, hard laugh and turn to leave.

He calls out to me. "Wait."

But I just ignore him. He's not worth my time or my anger. I need to find Claire anyway.

Chapter Five

I move fast, needing to get away, and realize that I'm heading toward the stables. After walking the stone path to the wooden building, I head to the pasture and find that Ares is still there.

He trots over to me and nudges me with his head.

I smile. "Hey, boy. I didn't expect you to still be here."

He snorts and stomps.

Laughing, I pet his head. I swear, I feel connected to him in some way.

Footsteps alert me that we aren't alone. I turn and find Claire and Lydia making their way to the palace. Claire is dressed in a nice but simple brown dress, and Lydia is wearing an elegant blue one. They are riding together in silence, but both appear relaxed.

Soon, they find me in the field.

Lydia has the largest smile I've ever seen on her face.

They make their way over and tie up the horses.

Lydia heads to me and wraps her arms around me.

"My dear child, I've missed you so much. I've been awaiting your arrival."

I deepen our hug, because I find that I've missed her riddling ways. "I've missed you, too."

She pulls back and cups my face with her hand, her beautiful red hair reflecting in the sunlight. It's hard to fathom that it was over a year ago when she trained me in secret at the old family home. Her teachings helped me gain control over my increasing powers.

"Well, today, everything will be as it should. I can't wait to watch it happen." She grins, rubbing my arms.

I glance over at Claire.

She winks at me and holds back a laugh. Her blonde hair is pulled back into a loose ponytail, and her blue eyes are sparkling with mirth.

Despite their ride, Lydia doesn't have a hair out of place. I pull her back into a hug. "Are you training today?"

She pulls me closer once more. "Oh, no. I'm attending the ball tonight. I hear the King of Noslon may marry tonight."

I snort and pull back. "That's the rumor."

Looping her arm through mine, Claire approaches, tugging me toward the palace. "Speaking of the ball, we need to head back and get dressed. We must look our best for tonight."

Lydia motions for us to keep going. "Yes, go. I will see you both tonight."

We continue on our way, and as soon as we break away from the stables and are closing in on the quarters, Claire turns to me. "It was the strangest thing. I went to my parents' house to grab something this morning, and on my way out to return, Lydia was just standing outside the house, waiting on me. We rode in together, but we didn't talk. However, I could hear her mumbling to herself. It was the strangest thing that has ever happened to me."

I chuckle and pat her arm. "Welcome to the Knova I've always known."

Her body shakes with laughter, and she nods. "That's what I was thinking."

We walk through the door, making our way back into the quarters to find Mer and Mother are sitting on the couch. Mother's red hair is put into place, but her eyes are red from crying. Maybe I shouldn't have left her that way earlier, but I'm tired of being treated like the naïve girl I once was.

Rising from the couch, Mer sternly looks at me. "Where have you been? Do you know how much time you've wasted? It's lunch time, and we still haven't picked out your dress." She spreads her arms out. "Why would you do this to me?"

Can she pull back the drama? "Yes, this is all about you. I'm so sorry for being inconsiderate."

She snaps her fingers at me in anger. "My sister only gets married one time. This is a big deal for me. How could you be this way?"

Claire rubs her lips with her finger tips. "Um… she's not your sister until after she marries your brother."

Placing her hand over her heart, Mer glances at me. "Hey, she's been my sister for a year now."

I wrap my arms around her. "Yes, we are sisters. Calm down. Let's eat, and I promise to be a good girl."

She sighs and pats my cheek. "That's all I'm asking. Just behave and do what I say. Let's eat, and if you continue to be nice, we may just have a surprise for you."

I snort. "We? I'm scared. Maybe I won't behave."

I glance back at my mother, who is watching but is still upset from earlier. She appears to still have tears in her eyes. I walk over to her and reach out my hand. "Want to help me make something in the kitchen? If Mer doesn't eat at regular intervals, she gets demanding."

She startles and glances at my friend. "This isn't her being demanding?"

Claire chuckles.

Mer crosses her arms.

I sigh. "No, it isn't."

Mother gets up, and we walk into the kitchen.

I leave my two friends behind, hoping they can start to get to know one another. They have many similarities. They are both loyal, dependable, and amazing women. However, Claire is more of an observer and listener, while Mer doesn't have a filter. I love them both, but for different reasons.

I'm looking through the cupboard when Mother turns to me.

She sniffs and rubs her nose. "I'm sorry. I was out of line. I just don't want to see you get hurt more than you've already been. You're my daughter, and I love you very much. It's a miracle just to be able to talk to and see you."

I lean over and kiss her on the cheek. "I get it. We are all kind of emotional. I never thought I'd get to see you again, and I've missed you so much." I turn back to the cupboard. "Now, what are we going to make?"

Coming next to me, she pulls out the ingredients needed for pancakes, my favorite. She walks to the counter and starts mixing the ingredients together. "I figure we should have breakfast for lunch."

I'm not going to argue on that. "Yes, that works for me."

We work together, and soon, the kitchen smells like cinnamon and vanilla.

I wink at her. "Within ten seconds, Mer is going to walk in."

She grins. "She has no manners, does she?"

Movement comes from the den, and Mer pops her head in, sniffing, her jade eyes searching. "What in Knova is that? I must have it now."

Claire walks in behind her and comes over to nudge me. "I take it we are having pancakes?"

Pulling out plates, Mother distributes the pancakes amongst us.

Mer grabs hers and scurries to the kitchen table. She's already digging into hers before the three of us can join her. She points her fork at me. "You've hidden too much delicious food from me. How could you not tell me about these amazing pancakes? These are way better than what they serve at the dining hall."

I scratch my head. "We don't cook in Noslon."

She takes another huge bite and talks with her mouth full. "I know. We need to remedy that. I can't go back to not having this."

Claire snorts and begins eating.

Mother snickers and reaches out to pat Mer's arm.

"I'm glad you enjoy it. This is Ari's favorite, too. I'll make a point to make this again soon."

We all dig in, and the food is delicious. Soon, we are all finished.

Laying down her fork, Claire perks up. "Is it dress-picking time?"

"Yes!" Mer squeals, clapping her hands.

We all rise, and I carry our dirty dishes to the sink.

The three of them have taken off to my room, and there is a lot of commotion.

Oh, dear goodness. Do I want to join them? I glance toward the front door. It would be so easy to sneak…

"Ariah, get your butt in here," Mer's voice rings in my ears.

I sigh. I was so close to freedom. I head to my bedroom door and force myself to enter.

Mer is holding up a black dress, and Claire and Mother are shaking their heads.

Claire digs through a few dresses. "No, why would she wear black? She needs to wear a bold red or blue."

Laying down the dress on top of several other black ones, Mer glances at the inventory. "She said to bring something Noslon, and well, this is us. We wear black."

Digging through the pile, Mother pulls out a few yellow gowns. "Well, she's from Agrolon. So, if she's trying to represent a kingdom, she should be wearing yellow."

Claire glances over at me.

Mer's forehead is creased. She crosses her arms, scowling at my mother. "She may have been raised here, but Noslon is her home."

What in Knova is going on? I'm not sure I can take it much longer.

Claire comes over and squeezes my hand.

I glance up at her, at a loss for what to do.

She winks at me, then walks back to the bed and smiles. "Let's be honest. Ari is different. Despite being raised in a kingdom where the king despised her, she grew up kind and moral. Then, she got cast away in a sense by the king and found another home in Noslon." She looks up and taps her lips with her fingertip. Her eyes light up. "Wait… I have the perfect dress."

She runs to my closet and digs through it. Of course, she'd have gotten to know my closet in my absence.

Mother chuckles.

Joining the search, Mer edges over next to her.

After a few minutes, Claire squeals. "Here it is." She pulls out a stunning, white long-sleeve dress that has black lace woven into the top and all the way down the waist. "See, white to represent her heart, and the black woven in signifies her allegiance to Noslon."

Mer reaches out and strokes it in admiration.

Looking at the gown with reverence, Mother nods. "That is perfect."

I pull her into my arms and squeeze. "I agree, for once. Good job."

Mer pulls me toward her and places the dress in my hands. "Go change. We need to hurry."

I glance at the time. It's just after lunch time. Why is she being stranger than normal?

She waves her hands toward the dress. "Put the damn thing on."

What the hell is her problem? I am about to kick them out of the room, so I can change until I take another look at the dress. I'm going to need help zipping it up, so I just steel myself.

Claire takes the dress from me, and I strip down to my underwear, making sure my tattoo is hidden from her and mother. I don't want to have to address this right now.

Claire unzips the dress and has it on the floor for me to step into.

When I lift the dress up my body, holding it in place, Mer comes behind and zips it up.

I'm surprised at how well the dress fits me, as if it was made for this occasion.

Claire is smiling brightly. "You look beautiful."

Tugging my hands, Mer leads me to sit on the bed.

Mother brings over the eyeshadow and reaches for a blanket. "Here. Wrap this around you. We don't want to get the makeup all over your white gown."

Smacking herself on the head with the palm of her hand, Mer looks chastised. "I should have thought of that. Yes, do not get makeup on this gown."

Claire comes over to sit on the other side of me and gives me a reassuring smile. "It'll be over before you know it."

Groaning, Mer glares at me. "I know. I hate her. She looks so beautiful without makeup, but today, we are adding more than usual. All right, let's work."

I sit, attempting to be still while all three ladies debate on my makeup. It's determined to put light charcoal on my eyes, a light pink blush on my cheeks, and blood-red lipstick on my lips. While Mer applies my makeup, Claire paints my nails the same dark red color as my lipstick.

Watching them with a frown, Mother sits on the bed. When all is said and done, she walks over. "It's my turn. I get to do her hair."

Mer opens her mouth to object.

But I lean over and pinch her arm. "Move it. Mother gets a turn, too."

She narrows her eyes. "I don't like sharing stuff. I'm used to having you all to myself."

Laughter bubbles out before I can contain it. "I love you. Having them here doesn't diminish that. I appreciate you taking time to do my makeup."

She reaches over and pats my arm. "All right, fine." She turns to my mother. "Do her hair. I have to go get ready anyways. I'll be back soon."

She rises and blows me a kiss before making her way out the door.

Turning back, Mother looks at Claire and me. "She's blunt and odd. I like her, but she's a lot to handle."

I chuckle. "You have no idea."

Giggling, Claire points to my hair. "Come on, let's get to working on her hair. From what I've heard, Owen has a surprise for her soon, and we all need to be ready for the ball to happen soon after."

Mother grins and begins brushing my hair. After a few minutes, I realize what she's planning on doing.

She's curling my hair and leaving it long. When my hair is done, she bends down in front of me. "You look beautiful."

I grin and stand to look in the mirror. When I first see

my reflection, I don't recognize myself. My hair is dark and has loose curls following through to the ends. My gray eyes stand out against the light gray eyeshadow and eyeliner, and I have a slight ethereal tone. My lips stand out against my pale skin and make a striking contrast to the rest of my makeup. The key is around my neck. For once, I feel like I look like a queen. I smile and turn to look at them. "Thank you both so much."

Claire smiles and grabs Mother's hand. "Come on, we need to hurry and get ready."

They hurry out of my room, and for once, their actions make me feel like a stranger. In the past, the three of us always got ready together, but this time, they've left me.

There is a light knock at the door, and I turn to find Jacob standing at the threshold. His blonde, short hair is groomed to perfection, and he's wearing black dress clothes. He fidgets and pulls at the collar around his neck.

I laugh. "Are you okay?"

Pulling once more at the collar, he sighs in defeat. "No, but this is what Mer said I had to wear."

I bite my lip. "You do realize that you don't have to listen to her?"

He stares at the ground, avoiding me.

I walk over to him and place my hand on his arm. "It's okay. It's kind of obvious you have a crush on her."

His face jerks up. "What? How'd you know?"

I grin. "I think you would make a great couple. You balance her."

Fidgeting, he taps his foot. "Owen would kill me. It can't happen... her and me."

I tilt my head to the side and take in his pained expression. "You leave him to me."

He grins. "I'll take your word for it, but we need to go. They are all waiting."

Mother's bedroom door opens, and she and Claire come walking out.

I'm surprised to see them dressed in their formal clothes, with their make-up and hair finished in such a short amount of time. Claire is wearing a light blue A-line dress that fits her perfectly, and Mother is wearing a yellow gown that contrasts with her red hair.

Mother smiles. "Oh, we thought we heard you. Jacob, is it time?"

He nods and heads toward the door.

I look around. What's going on?

Claire moves beside me and takes my hand. She smiles and places a pair of yellow glass earrings in my hand. "I went home this morning to get these for you to wear today. That way, your home kingdom is represented as well. They've been in my family for decades, and it seems fitting that my sister would wear them on her wedding day."

My vision gets blurry, and I wipe away the moisture the best I can before my make-up gets ruined. I put the earrings in my ears with shaky hands and squeeze her hand. "Thank you so much. It means a lot."

As soon as I take a step back, Mother pulls me into her arms as well. "We need to hurry, but I want you to know that I love you."

Jacob clears his throat. "Come on, ladies, we need to get going in order to get back in time for the ball."

I glance at them. "What are we doing? Do I need to change?"

"No!" they all shout at once.

Okay, this is getting strange.

Jacob walks next to me and guides me to the door, with Mother and Claire following behind. We continue to walk, and I realize that we are making our way to the stables.

I turn around. "What's going on?"

Mother glances at Jacob, and Claire is biting her lip.

I sigh. They aren't going to tell me anything.

Mother grins. "We are just going to town for a minute. That's all."

"In our dresses?" I am at a loss for words. What in Knova is going on?

They don't answer, so we continue our trek down. I notice that the Noslon carriage is pulling out of the stables.

Glancing behind us, Jacob opens the door. "Hurry, ladies. We don't want the Agrolon King stopping us."

I don't know what's going on, but I'm all for getting away for a little while. This place doesn't feel like home anymore.

He hurries inside the carriage, shutting the door.

I glance and realize that Logan is our driver. This is completely odd.

We pull out of the gate, and when I glance back, there are a ton of guards trying to catch up to us. However, they are just on foot, and Logan has us moving fast. We bounce in the carriage, but I'm not going to complain. After a while, the village comes into view and the carriage slows to a much slower pace.

After a few minutes, I realize we are going around town and should be coming up on Claire's parents' house soon. Where are they taking me? What if Owen starts looking for me? I guess, since Jacob is involved, he must be aware but that doesn't seem like him.

Each person is avoiding eye contact with me, so something strange is going down. If I didn't trust them all, I'd be going crazy.

We pull up at Claire's, and the carriage comes to a rolling stop. Jacob jumps out and turns around to help us out of the carriage.

When we get out, Logan comes over, his black hair tousled from the ride, and grimaces. "You look beautiful."

I attempt to smile at him. "Thanks, just a little sore after that ride."

Looking around, Jacob heads away from Claire's.

What is he doing? "Hey, where are you going?"

He ignores me, continuing on his path.

Logan takes Claire's hand. "He wants to see the old Pearson house. Come on."

They have all lost their minds. Why are we dressed up in our finest outfits, traipsing around the forest? I feel as if I'm channeling Mer right now.

They all walk off ahead of me, and I come to my senses. Otherwise, I'm going to be left behind. I hurry to catch up, and before long, we are following the worn path to the Pearson house. "How is this path still worn?"

Logan glances back, his forehead creased. "I don't

know. It's been like this the entire time. Even with the grass dying and weeds sprouting, the path remains clear."

This place has always been strange.

We continue our pace, and as soon as the Pearson house clearing comes into view, the power comes close to knocking me off my feet. I push the power out and make my way to the clearing.

Once the house comes into view, I stop in my tracks. Even though the trees in the rest of the kingdom are wilting, those here in the yard seem to be flourishing. Their branches are full of green leaves and have fragrant pink flower buds all over. The grass surrounding the house is lush and green, and the air smells clean and fresh.

However, the blossoming vegetation isn't what catches my eye.

Owen is in the middle of the open space, wearing his royal Noslon attire and crown which I've never seen him in. Willow is standing beside him, dressed in all black, wearing the Queen's crown with a huge smile across her face. Mer is behind Owen, wearing her royal attire and crown, holding a dagger.

Focusing on me, Owen holds out his hand.

I walk to him without any hesitation. When I reach him, he takes my hand. I look around and glance back at my family and Jacob. "What's going on?"

Owen gently grabs my chin and turns my face so that I'm looking at him. "You were serious about getting married, right?"

Oh, my goodness. I glance around, and everything comes together. "I thought we were getting married at the ball?"

He raises an eyebrow. "If I remember correctly, you said that if Elizabeth touches me again you're gone. I can't have that, and she'll try as soon as we enter the ballroom. I want us to walk in united. And, to be honest, I don't want to get married in that stuffy palace. I'd rather marry you right here."

I grin and my heart quickens. "Okay. I'm in."

Mer giggles. "Hell yeah, and I get to be the officiant."

"Oh, dear goodness." My mother flinches in the background.

I have to bite my tongue to keep from laughing out loud.

Mer ignores them and smiles at us. "I never thought my brother would get married. He's too controlling, ornery, and unbending. He likes to tell people what to do and hates being challenged."

Owen shakes his head. "Really, Mer? We're doing this now?"

Pointing the dagger at Owen, she places her other hand on her hip. "Let me finish." She clears her throat and licks her lips. "Now, like I was saying. He's controlling, ornery, and unbending. Sometimes, you can't be around him because he's a little too much. However, that has changed ever since he met you." She looks at me and smiles. "The day you walked into our village, well, you caused a lot of trouble. But, for once, Owen had found his match. He used to never smile, but now, I see it on a daily basis. So, what I'm saying is, that we, Queen Willow and I, accept you into our family."

She hands the dagger to Owen and comes over to give me a hug. She steps aside and stands next to her mother.

Owen takes the dagger and looks at me. "You complete me in a way I never knew I needed. I promise to always be by your side and love you until death." He pulls out a ring made of dark gold that is just a set of thorns wrapping around. He puts in on my finger and looks me in the eye. "I love you."

Making his way to my side, Jacob hands me a ring I didn't know he had. It's similar to my wedding band but thicker, more fitting for a man.

I look into Owen's eyes. "Everything I've gone through has led me to you. You believe in me and make me a stronger person. I know, with you by my side, we can overcome any obstacle in our way. I promise to always be by your side and love you until death."

He grins as I put the ring on his finger.

Willow moves to the position where Mer was. She looks at me. "It's custom in our kingdom that, once an official wedding ceremony takes place, the King's wife is officially the Queen. Since I'm alive, I must give the blessing before you make your oath. So, I give you my blessing and step down from the throne." She removes the crown from her head and holds it in her hands.

Turing back to me, Owen uses the dagger to cut his hand. "Since you aren't from Noslon, we must mix our blood before you can receive the crown and we can be wed. That way, our blood runs through you."

I take the dagger. "What is it with you all and cutting?" I wince as I cut my hand, blood dripping on the ground.

He smiles at me and clasps our hands together, where our blood mixes and our wounds are touching.

Reaching for the dagger, Willow cleans the blade with

her dress. "Repeat after me. I pledge my life to you and promise to take care of one another as well as the residents of Noslon. I will honor and protect those of my blood and heart."

I project to Owen. *Just Noslon? Why wouldn't we want to protect all of Knova?*

He grins. *You're right.*

We both look at each other.

I can feel his power more than ever with our blood truly mixing.

We say together, "I pledge my life to you and promise to take care of one another as well as the residents of Knova. I will honor and protect those of my blood and heart."

When those words leave our lips, Owen bends to seal our promise with a kiss. As soon as his lips touch mine, power like never before surges through me.

I gasp at the sheer raw strength. The wind blows and the earth shakes. People are gasping, but I can't focus on them.

Lightning crashes down around us, and our families back away.

The power latches onto me and seeps into my being, becoming one with my own. The wind begins to calm and the ground stills.

Owen and I turn to check on the others, and they are all standing there with their mouths open and awe on their faces.

I look over at Owen and realize he's glowing. What the hell is going on?

Rattling echoes around us, and I realize it's coming from the chest that I had found at the cave a while ago.

Willow walks over. "I felt like I needed to bring it, and it's a good thing I did." She reaches down, scoops it up, and brings it over to me. The chest is shaking harder the closer it gets to me.

Mother rushes over. "What is that?"

I glance at her. "We aren't sure. I found it in the Noslon village a while ago; however, it wouldn't let me open it then."

Huddling into Jacob's side, she points to the box. "Well, open it up. I want to see."

I glance at Owen, not sure if I should.

He nods. *It's time to find out what's in there.*

Okay, let's do this. I remove the key from around my neck and slip it into the keyhole. For the first time, it clicks. I open it and gasp when I see what's inside.

Owen grabs the chest and takes it away, ready to see what's inside, but it rattles worse once he pulls it away.

Willow reaches over and plucks it out of his hands then places it back into mine. "That is meant for her. Stop taking it away."

Mer inches closer. "What is it?"

I take a deep breath and pull the most beautiful crown out of the velvet-lined interior. It's made of pure gold and has two stones in it, but it looks as if two are missing. There is a black stone that must represent Noslon that's already embedded, and there is a yellow stone of Agrolon. I pick up the crown, and it begins shaking. "What the hell do I do?"

Willow comes closer and takes it from me, putting it on my head.

As soon as it makes contact with my scalp, I feel a comforting warmth descend all down my body. My vision goes dark. There are gasps from those around me, but I can't see what's going on. I blink hard, and when I open my eyes, it seems as if a veil has been lifted from my eyes. The world seems more sharp and cohesive. When I look around, I see shock written on my family's faces. "What's wrong?"

Owen grins and touches my face. "Nothing at all. But I think we're truly about to cause more hell than we realized."

I tilt my head as my brother approaches.

As soon as I'm within an arm's length away, he's reaching up to touch my face.

My power jumps out at him, and his green eyes take on a glow similar to how Willow's does on occasion.

Willow chuckles. "I never would have dreamed this, but you do realize what this means?"

I turn to her and shake my head.

The grin on her face is one like a big secret is being revealed. "That crown... that's the Savior's crown, and it wanted on your head. You're the one."

My mother gasps and falls to her knees.

Mer's eyes widen, and Jacob smirks.

Claire, however, is silent. She doesn't seem surprised like the rest. Her blue eyes hold my gaze.

Running a hand through his hair, my brother looks puzzled. "That's impossible. It's supposed to be the second ascended."

Mer snaps out of her stupor and bounces on her feet. "She *is* the second ascended."

What the hell is she talking about? Only women, except for Owen, ever reach Enlightenment.

We all turn to her, and Jacob sighs. "Out with it, Mer."

Despite the whole situation, I'm proud of Jacob for kind of speaking up.

She zones in on Logan. "You have power. That makes Ariah the second."

I forgot about that. She did tell me that in the woods, but I've been so preoccupied.

He takes a step back. "I have no clue what you're talking about. I'm a man, for goodness sakes."

Oh, this is going to be fun. Mer opens her mouth, but I want to be the one to tell him.

"Mer can tell who has power and how strong it is. She sees it in you."

His head snaps in my direction.

Of course, Owen, Mer, and Jacob don't react since they already know about Mer's ability. I'm not surprised that Willow isn't shocked. I mean, she seems to know a lot somehow. She's so much like Lydia and Hazel.

However, Claire's eyes widen at this, and my mother's face has gone pale white.

Logan growls. "Well, she must be wrong this time."

Marching over, Mer points at him. "Listen, I get you don't trust us, and that's an admirable quality, but your sister does. Now, I know that used to not mean anything. I mean, she'd trust anyone, but I digress."

Wow, that was below the belt even if it was true. "Thanks. I appreciate that."

Owen chuckles and gets closer, putting his arm around my waist and pulling me to his side.

Mer glances back at me. "This isn't about you. Well, it kind of is, but you know what I mean." She huffs and turns her attention back to my brother. "Like I was saying before I got interrupted, we know you have power. And Ariah told us that you are bonded to her."

Glaring, Logan steps toward me. "We swore we'd never tell."

Claire sighs, disappointment on her face.

Looking devastated, Mother gasps. "Is this true?"

Why is there always drama in my life? I hate drama and try to stay away from it, but somehow, it always finds me. I'm so tired of hiding and sick of always feeling guilty. I made poor and naïve choices in the past, but not anymore. "Yes, it's true, and this is my family. All of you are my family now. I'm done hiding. The more we keep secrets and hide, the more King Percy is winning. He has torn us apart, and I will not stand for it anymore."

Mother's face is now streaming with tears.

Claire comes over and takes my hand. She turns to Logan. "She is right. I've guessed you guys were hiding something from the beginning, but I didn't push it. I knew you were trying to protect me, but it has torn us apart further." She glances over at Logan, Mer, and Willow, smiling at them. "I didn't know what to think when you first arrived, but I'm glad you found her. I can tell you all truly care for her, and that makes me trust you." Claire turns to face Logan. "It's time to accept she has a husband and accept these people as your family. We have to start doing something different or King Percy will win."

My crown takes on a shine, and I glance over at my other half. "He won't win. I'll die before I let him."

Owen grins and turns me so I'm facing him. He cups my cheek in his hand. "We won't let him win, and I won't let you die. You are the Savior. This has been your fight all along."

I always felt at the center of the prophecy, but I thought I was the extra. The means to get to the Savior. However, in this moment, I know Owen and Willow are right. I'm the Savior, and I will not let Knova fall into ruin because of a selfish, arrogant man.

I gaze straight into Owen's eyes. "Let the games begin."

Chapter Six

✦

We arrive back at the palace, and the guards welcome us at the gate. The older one in front paces as he waits for us to exit the carriage.

Owen gets out first and turns to help me.

I'm glad I've taken off the crown and hidden it back inside the box.

"King Owen. King Owen," the guard repeats, trying to gain my husband's attention.

I can't contain my stupid grin. He is mine in every way.

Owen ignores him and rolls his eyes, but I'm the only one who can see him do that. I try to contain my laugh, but it almost slips out.

The guard comes closer. "King Owen, King Percy was worried that you had left without a word. He has requested your presence in the throne room immediately."

The rest of the party climbs out, and since Jacob drove the carriage this time, he walks and joins us.

Owen turns around to face the guard. "King Percy does not rule me. I am here as a potential ally, not as a citizen of Agrolon. I'm busy, but I will make sure to stop and talk to him at the ball."

The guard is standing there frozen, looking around, speechless. I feel kind of bad for him. He's just doing his job.

Owen takes my hand, and we walk past the guard whose mouth has dropped open. The others follow behind, and we are at my mother's quarters within minutes.

Mer laughs as soon as she walks through the door. "I think that guard was about to combust. He had no clue what to do."

Chuckling, Claire plops on the couch. "I know, but I do feel bad for him. I'm sure he's going to get in trouble with the king."

Logan sighs. "I see we are ready to shake things up right away." He looks at me, concern etched all over his face. "Are you sure you know what you're doing?"

I take a deep breath. I don't want to lie. "Nope, but I know that I can't let him win. Knova's fate depends on it."

He runs his hand through his hair and glances at Claire. She nods in encouragement.

He takes her hand. "Okay, let's do this." He glares at Owen. "However, if something happens to Ari, I'm blaming you."

Owen laughs, which surprises the hell out of me. He

doesn't laugh for many people. "If something happens to her, you can beat me."

Logan purses his lips. "All right, it's a deal."

Glancing around, I realize it's almost time to go.

Mer rushes toward me. "And it's time for you to change."

I look down at my outfit. "What's wrong with this dress? I love it."

Walking over, Mother says sadly, "It looks like a wedding dress, but you're walking in to declare war."

What? Why would she say that? "No, I'm not."

Jacob is standing in the corner but steps into the den. "What do you think is going to happen tonight? He plans on seeing Princess Elizabeth married off to Owen."

That's true. I guess, I knew we weren't going to let them manipulate us, but I didn't think about it as declaring war.

Owen's eyes have concern laced through them. "Are you ready?"

I can do this. It's my destiny, right? "Yes, I'm ready for this."

Mer squeals. "Then, it's time to find you a kickass dress."

I blow out through my mouth. I thought I had been through this part of the day.

All of us ladies walk into my room, leaving the men outside in the den. I guess, I'm not the only one who needs a wardrobe change.

Mer pulls out a solid black, lace dress that has thin sleeves and crisscrosses in the front. At the waist, it flows down in several layers. My necklace looks perfect with the dress, but I worry about my tattoos.

Coming up beside me, Mother touches the material. "Oh, this is beautiful."

I smile, but I can't help worrying. Mother hasn't seen our tattoos yet, and she's struggling to adapt.

Mer glances back and pulls out some long-sleeved gloves that will ride up my arm.

I sigh in relief. I think she needs more time to acclimate.

Willow moves toward me and pulls me into a tight embrace. "I am so glad to have you as my daughter. You will look royal and beautiful. This is your right." She turns and takes my mother's hand. "I could sure use a cup of coffee."

Mother's face lights up. "Oh, me too. Let's go grab a cup while we wait on Ari."

Once they leave out the door, I turn back to the dress. I peel the one I'm in off.

Claire sucks in a deep breath, causing her to cough. I look up and notice that her eyes are firmly on my tattoo.

She points. "What's that?"

Mer walks over to her and hits her on the back hard.

I take a step toward them. "What are you doing?"

She continues hitting Claire, and Claire keeps hacking. "She's choking. I'm helping her."

What in Knova? Is she serious?

Moving away, Claire clears her throat. "I'm good. Thanks for helping." Her gaze zooms back to my tattoos. "When did you get those? They're amazing, but I'm not sure what they signify."

I look down at them as well and trace the design with my fingertip. "Well, I don't want to overwhelm Logan and Mother at once, but Owen and I are soulmates."

Her eyes are about to pop out of her face. "What? How do you know?"

I look up. "Because he has a matching one, and we can mind-speak to one another."

Her forehead creases. "Mind-speak?"

I grab the gloves from Mer and begin putting them on. "Yes, we can talk to each other mentally."

Claire gasps. "Are you serious?"

Laughing, Mer plops on the bed. "Yes, she is, but she's awful at it. She can't remember that she can do that for the life of her."

I throw my hands up. "It's not something I've grown up doing."

Mer rolls her eyes. "It's been a year. Maybe you should practice."

I purse my lips. "Yes, maybe Owen and I should only talk to each other that way when we're around you."

Her head snaps up, her eyes wide. "You better not. You can't exclude me."

I shrug my shoulders. "Well, you did just tell me to practice."

She puts her hand over her heart. "But not at my expense. I need to know what's going on."

Laughing, Claire fixes the glove on my right hand. "You guys bicker like siblings. I'm so glad to have another sister in the mix."

Mer's face lights up. "I guess we are all sisters. You're right."

A sudden knock at the door interrupts us, and Mer walks over to yank the door open.

Jacob is standing there and takes a step back in shock.

She puts her hand on her hip. "Can we help you?"

He grins. "No, but we need to be heading out. It's time for the show."

Turning toward me, she motions me ahead. We all walk out into the den to join the rest of our group.

Owen comes over and wraps his arm around me, brushing his lips over mine.

Just then, Mother clears her throat, not thrilled with our display.

Owen pulls back and winks. He turns to the front of the room. "Are you guys ready?"

They all nod, but Mother's face loses its color and Logan appears unhappy. They don't understand, but I don't expect them to. This life, this unfair ruling under King Percy, is all they have ever known.

I put my arm through Owen's, and we head out the door. Just then, I remember something. I turn and face the others. "They will expect Mer to have a date, so Jacob, can you help out?"

Jacob's eyes widen.

Frowning, Mer glares at me. "I can find my own dates, princess."

I shrug. "You don't deserve him anyway."

She moves beside him, pulling him flush against her. "Like hell I don't."

I snicker and turn back to the front.

Owen is looking at me with a strange expression, but I just shrug and keep on the path to the ballroom.

The closer we get to the ballroom, the more frantic my heart pounds. Facing the Agrolons and Orlons has to be done, but I'm just not sure how to go about it. I'm the Savior, not Emerson. This is hard to fathom, seeing as for my first nineteen years, I was convinced it was my sister.

Owen squeezes my hand. *I'll be with you the whole time. It's your time to shine. Don't let them make you think otherwise.*

I take a deep breath. He's right, as always.

We walk through the hallway and reach the entryway to the ball. It's in full swing, and Owen bends down and wraps his arm around me.

Taking point on my other side, Willow appears, and she's holding the wooden box from earlier.

What is she doing? I don't want it here. "Why did you bring that?"

She grins and touches my arm. "I'm sorry, but I had to. It begins. You will make me proud."

She walks off and heads into the back of the ballroom. To my utter astonishment, she walks straight to Lydia and they begin talking.

What the hell? I always thought they could be sisters, but to see them interacting as if they know one another still comes as a shock.

Owen tugs me toward the front.

King Percy has already zeroed in on us. Nick, Emerson, and my father are standing with him. The King and Nick are wearing nice royal outfits, and my father is dressed very well. Emerson is wearing a red gown that enhances the darkness of her hair. It's funny, because it almost looks black like mine against her gown.

We make our way to them.

King Percy has rage clear on his face. "Well, King Owen, I'm surprised to find that you are accompanied by someone."

Looking down at me, Owen grins. "I am lucky."

My father grunts and sticks his hand out in Owen's direction. "I'm Gabe." He points to my sister. "This here is Emerson, the Savior. I'm both her and Ariah's father."

Owen stiffens. Being my father is not a good thing in Owen's mind.

I can feel Nick's eyes, watching me.

Emerson moves toward me and envelops me in a huge hug. She buries her face in my hair. "I thought you were dead."

I pull back and look in the king's eyes. "That's not the only time I've defied death."

Groaning, Owen frowns. "Really? We're making this a joke now?"

Nick advances toward me, but Owen blocks him.

Nick's eyes widen, and he stands up a little straighter.

Turning around, Emerson walks over to him.

King Percy comes closer, and the smell of oranges once again infiltrates my nose, but I ignore my upset stomach. He looks behind me and motions someone to come over. Within seconds, someone wedges themselves between Owen and me.

What the hell is going on? I turn to find Elizabeth there, hanging all over Owen. She's wearing the kingdom's yellow color in a fancy, flowy dress. "Oh, King Owen, you look very handsome tonight. How about allowing me to have the first dance with you?"

Laughter bubbles out of me. Does she think there is an actual chance with him? He's all mine.

Owen detangles himself from her evil clutches. "No, I'm good. I promised my wife all the dances here tonight."

King Percy and Princess Elizabeth become very still.

My father sucks in a breath. "You're married?"

Clenching his fist, King Percy glares. "Your wife? I thought you were marrying my daughter this night?"

Owen smiles and walks around Elizabeth, coming back to stand at his place beside me. He kisses my lips and pulls me close. "Why would I marry her when I have this beautiful woman by my side?"

Elizabeth hisses. I knew she was a snake.

She gets in his face. "You will just have to undo it. You are meant to be mine. Don't be stupid and align yourself with her."

Sam's voice comes up from behind King Percy and Gabe. "Oh, I thought you were promised to me."

The king turns to face him, only to find Sam's parents are also there beside him.

The Queen of Orlon is attempting to appear calm, but her nostrils are flaring.

King Michael has a look of forced indifference on his face.

Scowling, Sam is standing there with his arms crossed.

They are all dressed formally in their standard emerald green.

Elizabeth walks over to Sam and puts her arm through his, but he drops it and takes a step away.

King Percy raises his hands in front of his chest. "Now, come on. Of course she is yours. We were just hoping that

King Owen might be persuaded more if there was a chance at Princess Elizabeth's hand."

King Michael narrows his eyes at the Agrolon King. "You didn't think that's something you should have discussed with me?"

Snarling, King Percy lifts his chin. "Why would I need to do that? I have the Savior locked in to me."

Oh, wow. I can't believe this is happening.

The Queen of Orlon moves in close to him. "We have been an ally and friend. You can't just do whatever you want."

King Percy tilts his head up. "Actually, I can." He turns and glares at me. "And now, I want you gone."

Knowing he's having a small meltdown brings a smile to my face. He's acting out in public. I guess he has gotten more arrogant during my absence. "I have just as much of a right to be here as my husband."

Owen intertwines our left hands together, showing our wedding bands to the Agrolon King.

Sam gasps, and Nick takes a step closer, almost like he can't believe what he sees.

My father groans and places his hand over his forehead. "What have you done?"

Emerson smiles at me.

I can feel Sam's parents watching me with their calculating eyes. I take a deep breath and stare my father down. "What have I done? I've married the man I love."

King Percy looks around and notices that we are causing a scene. He glares at me. "All right, let's all have some fun before the night is over. We can always discuss things later."

As we turn to the dance floor, Elizabeth stops us.

Taking her finger, she rubs it down Owen's chest. "Are you sure you don't want to dance with me?"

My blood is boiling. She has some nerve.

Owen grabs her wrist, dropping her hand down. "I'm positive."

Elizabeth's mouth drops open.

I smirk at her as we pass by. Maybe it will register that he is all mine and nothing will come between us.

We get on the dance floor, and Owen pulls me toward him, moving to the music.

Within seconds, Mer and Jacob are next to us. She grins. "What did we miss?"

Sighing, Owen places his forehead against mine. "You missed me having great restraint for once."

Jacob's face scrunches up in confusion. "What do you mean?"

Lifting his head back up, Owen looks at him. "I didn't kill King Percy, but I wanted to badly."

Mer shakes her head. "Yeah, that probably wouldn't be good right now. Maybe later, you'll get your chance."

Did she just say that right now? I look around. What is wrong with her? There are a ton of people around us. "People could hear you."

She shrugs her shoulder.

Of course she doesn't care—one thing I love about her.

Jacob is looking at her, smitten.

Owen glances at him as well and gives me a calculated look. I brush my lips on his, trying to distract him.

After several songs, someone taps Owen on the shoulder.

I glance up and cringe when I see it's Nick.

He clears his throat. "May I cut in?"

Glaring, Owen looks back at him. "Nope, you sure can't."

Nick flinches and stares at me.

Is he expecting me to do something about this? The last thing I want to do is dance with him. I shrug at him.

Owen changes directions, moving us across the floor from him. He pulls me closer and leans into my ear, his tone deep. "Why can't those two princes keep their eyes to themselves? I may have to teach them a lesson."

I giggle and cuddle even closer to him. "My heart is all yours, dear." He better not think otherwise, or I may have to hurt him.

He smiles against my neck. "It better be. You are mine in every single way now, and I don't share." He kisses my neck and I shudder.

We haven't had alone time in only a day, but it seems like forever. I moan and tremble at his attention. I'm caught off guard when I'm pulled back by my arm. I turn around and find Sam standing there, his hand still on me. "What the hell are you doing?"

Owen grabs him by the shirt and pushes him against the wall of the ballroom that we're next to. He holds Sam up by his shirt, getting in his face. "Do not touch her again."

Sam glares at him, not caring that he's at Owen's mercy. "She only is with you because she's scared for her life. You are a barbarian that doesn't play by the rules."

How could he think that? My mate isn't a barbarian.

He's someone in tune with nature and ethical. I'm so tired of people being so narrow-minded.

Scowling, Jacob appears by Owen's side. He looks at Sam. "Stop being jealous." He puts his hand on Owen's shoulder. "And you need to calm down. You're making a scene."

Before I can walk toward Owen to try to ease some of the attention, someone puts something over my mouth and nose, and the room turns black.

Chapter Seven

I come to and have no clue how long I've been passed out or where I am. I force my eyes open and blink at the bright light in the room. Once they are adjusted, I cringe. I'm in the king's chambers. Oh, hell no. The last time I was here, I almost died.

I try to sit up, but my head is woozy. I tilt back, almost falling, but catch myself in time. I take a deep breath and cringe. Owen must be freaking out. *Owen, are you there?*

He answers right away. *Ariah, where are you? I can't find you anywhere, but I'm close.*

Our connection is amazing, and at times like this, it's absolute perfection. The king doesn't realize we are bonded. Being stuck in this dark room isn't so bad when my husband can find me. *I'm in the royal chambers once again.*

His anger and concern fill our bond. *I'm on my way.*

Soon, I'll be out of this nightmarish place. A door

opens, and I turn to find both princes, kings, Elizabeth, and the Orlon Queen walking through the door.

King Michael pauses mid-step when he sees me. He turns to King Percy. "What is the meaning of this?"

Glaring at me, King Percy flares his nostrils. "She's a problem and a nuisance. It's time to get rid of her once and for all."

Nick walks in front of him. "No, Father. You can't do this. Think of all the repercussions."

Scowling at Nick, he focuses back to the King and Queen of Orlon. "See what I mean? She's managed to get both of our sons to act like fools."

Yes, I managed that. It was my intent all along. That way, I could be hurt repeatedly. What an idiot.

He grabs Nick's shirt and pulls him close. "All I know is that, when she left, you did as you were told with no trouble. As soon as she walked back inside my palace, all of you are acting foolish again. I don't know what it is about her, but it ends tonight."

Elizabeth stands next to her father. "Oh, please, let me do it. She's annoyed me since I first laid eyes on her. She stands out with her freakishly dark hair and pathetic ways. It's surprising that the stupid loud-mouthed princess has black hair, too. It must be because they are inbred."

What have I ever done to these people? My heart speeds up, and my breathing becomes shallow. I attempt to stand, but I'm still woozy from whatever they used to knock me out.

Elizabeth just laughs. "Don't worry, Raven. I put powder on you again, so you won't be able to do any harm." She walks over beside me and bends down. "Aren't you pathetic?"

Before it registers, I spit in her face.

She jerks her head back and wipes it off with the bottom of her dress. Then, she slaps me hard across my face.

Hot rage rises inside me, and my power begins pulsing even with the powder.

Owen's voice enters my head. *What the hell is going on? Are you okay?*

I want to answer him, but I can't lose focus right now. He's just going to have to get here.

Elizabeth raises her arm to slap me once more.

I push my power out and slam her against the wall.

King Percy's tone is desperate when he commands the guards. "Go fetch Lydia now."

Although she's trying to get down, Elizabeth doesn't move an inch. I still have her pinned against the wall. I'm stable enough to get up on my feet and turn to face the remaining royals.

The King and Queen of Orlon are stunned.

Rage is clear on King Percy's face.

I leer at him. "What have I ever done to you? Why have you always resented me so?"

He laughs hard. "Your mere presence insults me. The only reason you were here was for Emerson. The Savior is all I needed, and now that I have her, I can get rid of you with no problem. You and your family disgust me."

I chuckle hard. "Do you think you're worthy of leading Knova? You are a nasty, cruel tyrant that no one will want to follow."

Cringing, Nick's face is lined with concern. "What are you doing?"

I ignore him and focus on the man I hate. "I am tired of being pushed around. I am tired of your superior attitude. You will not treat me like this any longer."

King Percy moves fast and picks me up by my neck. "I don't care if no one wants to follow me. They will, because they'll have to." He begins putting pressure, restricting my air flow. "I am tired of this. That Noslon King put a false sense of confidence in you that I will end."

Walking beside him, King Michael touches his shoulder. "What are you doing?"

The Agrolon King focuses on me and smiles. "Finishing what I started over a year ago." He puts more pressure on my neck, restricting my air flow.

My power slips from me, allowing Elizabeth to get down. This isn't good. *Owen, I need you here now.*

Elizabeth comes over beside her father and snarls. "I want to watch her die."

I knew these people were cruel, but to what extent?

The queen's face is stark white. "No one needs to die. Just let her go. I'm sure she won't come back."

My vision is getting spotty, and my power is hindered by the powder and lack of oxygen. Right before the darkness overtakes me, Owen, Jacob, Lydia, and Willow walk through the door.

Owen's rage is evident on his face. His power surges, and he slams it into the king.

King Percy stumbles backwards from the force, releasing his hold on me.

I'm falling to the ground when thick arms catch me. I

look up and find that Jacob saved me from my tumble with the floor.

He stands me up and steadies me. "Are you okay?"

I nod my head and turn to find Owen.

He's circling the King of Agrolon. "Who do you think you are, harming my wife?"

Lydia and Willow hurry over to me.

Willow touches my neck. "Are you all right?"

Keeping my eyes on Owen, I jerk away. "I'm fine."

The Orlons and Nick have backed away, neither of them trying to help the king.

Looking around, Elizabeth's eyes land on Lydia. She takes a step toward her. "Do something now. That is your king."

Lydia lifts the box that contains my crown and glares at her.

Why the hell does she have that? It'd be nice if I were in on the plan.

She lifts her head high, and her voice echoes against the walls. "He's not my king any longer. King Owen is."

Distracted by her, Owen turns around and drops the king. "What the hell are you talking about?"

The king lands hard on his feet and attempts to hit Owen.

I come unhinged. No one hurts him.

My power blasts through me, raw and angry, and hits the king full force. I lift him in the air. There aren't wind gusts or a breeze, but I have him hovering five feet in the air.

Owen turns back around to face the king. I walk up

next to Owen. For the first time ever, I find fear in King Percy's eyes.

Turning to me, Elizabeth blasts power my way.

I shield myself and Owen, reflecting it back at her.

It hits her, and she falls to her knees, screaming in pain.

King Percy just stares down at me. "How is this possible? Emerson is not this strong."

I lower him, but my power keeps him stationary.

The box in Lydia's hands is trembling again.

Elizabeth's eyes flash to it. "What is that?"

Glancing back, I find that Lydia is walking toward me.

Taking advantage of the distraction, the king pulls out a dagger that had been hidden in his clothes and rushes me. He grabs me by the arm and pulls me back, piercing my skin with the blade.

Blood drips down my neck and onto my chest.

He huffs in disgust. "You think you're something, but you're not. I will kill you right here and now in front of them all. I will not have you messing up my plans. All you've ever been is a curse."

Owen's breathing hard and begins advancing.

The king laughs and uses me as a shield. "Take one step closer, and I'll slit her throat. You don't want that, now do you?"

Jacob grabs Owen's arm and drags him back.

Whimpering, Nick stands in the back, and our eyes meet.

Huh, is this how it ends? Beaten by the very man I hate that isn't worthy of leading Knova. All I've done is try to be kind and invisible, but that was not enough for him. He takes pleasure from beating us into submission, and Nick is just a reminder of who I use to be... of who I am being now. Do I want to die by his hands?

My power strengthens, reaching out and connecting with Owen.

As soon as he allows it in, the building increases.

It comes rushing up through my body, and I imagine the blade being pushed away from my neck. The king struggles to keep the dagger there, so I increase the flow.

I increase the power in small increments until the blade is off my neck and several inches away. I grab it and move both King Percy and I back to the wall. I have him pressed hard against the wall, and now, it's my turn to have the dagger to his neck.

His jaw drops and he tremors. "How is this possible? You're nothing."

I smile. "I guess you've always been mistaken about that."

The box's shaking increases, causing it to fall out of Lydia's hands. It's banging against the floor, desperate to open. After several seconds of this, the wood splits, and the crown slides across the floor, landing at my feet.

Queen Lora gasps. "Is that what I think it is?"

Owen hurries across the floor and picks it up. It strums in his hands, and the closer he gets to putting it on my head, the more the crown glows.

I drop my hands, but the king is too mesmerized to notice.

Right before it can be placed on my head, he reaches out and grabs it. When he makes contact, he howls in pain and releases it, dropping to his knees.

Placing it on my head, Owen steps back, a wide smile spreading across his face.

Elizabeth glares at me and comes over, trying to yank it off my head. "You don't deserve this."

Just like her father, when she touches it, she jerks back and falls to the ground in agony.

Owen reaches out to touch the wound on my neck, and he gulps. "Your wound is healed."

Yeah, I'm not surprised. At this point, crazy just seems to be the norm.

The King and Queen of Orlon make their way before me and bow.

I stumble back a step. I was wrong. This caught me off guard.

King Michael rises and looks at me. "I'm so sorry. We had no clue you were the Savior. I don't know how this is the case, but the crown is of legend. Only the Savior can wear it."

I tilt my head and take Owen's hand. "It shouldn't matter if I was the Savior or not. You should not treat anyone the way you all have treated me."

Looking at our joined hands, Sam smiles. "Remember, we took you in when you had nowhere to go."

Nick glares at the Orlons. "You knew she was alive and you didn't tell us?"

Sam pivots toward him. "No, you didn't deserve to know. You let him," he points to King Percy, "toss her over the balcony."

Growling, Owen pulls me closer to his side. "Enough. Neither of you deserve her or her kindness. You both betrayed her but in different ways. Only now, when you know she's the Savior, you have decided to play nice."

Crossing his arms, Jacob takes point on my other side. "Loyalty is earned, not entitled. That's one thing Ariah understands and one reason she is one of us. She is like a sister to me, and I will protect her at all costs. It isn't just Owen that feels this way."

This speech surprises me in many ways. One, Jacob is a man of few words, and he just said a lot for him. Secondly, he just called me his sister. Maybe he does like me, after all.

Running his hands down his face, Nick focuses on me. "She knows me. We've been friends forever. I've earned it."

I bark out a laugh. "You let me be tossed over a balcony."

Nick sighs. "I didn't know he would do that."

Taking a menacing step toward him, Owen growls. "That surprised you? He just had a blade to her throat."

This is escalating, and I need to get a handle on it before it explodes. I hold my hand up and look at Nick. "They are right. I don't trust you or any of the Orlons. However, we have to do something with them." I point over to where King Percy and Princess Elizabeth are recovering.

Someone enters the room and clears their throat.

I turn around and can't help the grin that spreads across my face. Pierce is here and alive. I drop Owen's hand and run over to hug him. "You're okay!"

He grins at me. "Thanks to you. I thought you might need some help, so I'm here to return the favor."

Moving behind me, Owen is standing close.

I turn and smile at him. "Pierce is the one who helped me get out of Orlon before Sam could kick me out."

Queen Lora flinches at this information but realizes her error and hides her emotions.

Sam shakes his head. "I wasn't kicking you out."

I raise an eyebrow. "Really? You thought I could just stay, even though you were engaged to Elizabeth?"

The queen clears her throat. "Obviously, we miscalculated, and we apologize. We will earn your favor."

Touching my arm, Pierce motions toward the Agrolon King and Princess. "Since you are the Savior, you can kick them out. They did try to kill you."

I glance back toward them.

Pure hatred is reflected on King Percy's face, and he moves in my direction.

Owen steps in front of me, blocking my view of the king. He growls. "Don't look at her. You aren't worthy. I should kill you."

I walk beside Owen and lean against him. "No, don't lower yourself to his standards."

King Percy and Elizabeth both burst out laughing.

She sneers at me. "You are so worthless. Why in Knova are you the Savior? This has to be a mistake." She glances behind me at Pierce. "Take her to the dungeon."

He smirks at her. "She is my queen. I will not take her anywhere she doesn't want to be."

Elizabeth's face becomes slack. "What did you just say?"

King Percy's eyes widen and he trembles. "This is my

kingdom, and you will do what I say. As my daughter stated, take her to the dungeon."

Moving toward the king, Owen rears back and punches him in the face.

He falls down hard on the floor, his lip split open. He groans and gets back on his feet, blood pouring down his face.

I glance back and notice that Willow, Lydia, and Pierce are side by side.

Jacob moves toward Owen, ready to help out.

Things are getting out of hand, and I don't want Owen to do something he will regret. "Please, calm down. We need to be rational."

Jacob glances back and lifts his hands.

Okay, yeah. Owen won't listen to that.

Sighing, Jacob focuses his attention back on his friend. "Instead of killing people, why don't you just let them stay overnight in the dungeon? That's more of a courtesy than they were going to bestow upon you. It will give us a full night to ponder what to do with them."

That has some merit, and at times like these, I'm reminded at how eloquent Jacob can be.

Owen pauses and he turns around to face us. He glances at me and cringes.

What the hell is that for? I glance around and realize people are waiting on me. Okay, this isn't awkward at all.

Chuckling, Owen enters my head. *Everyone is waiting on the command from you.*

My eyes widen, and I stare at him. *Why would they be waiting for me? You're the king.*

Despite everything, a smile breaks across his face. He

focuses on me. *I may be the king, but you are the Savior. You are the one destined to lead this country. Act like it.*

He's right, though I don't feel like a true leader. I glance over, and the Orlons are watching my every move, while Nick is trying to hide in the back. Elizabeth and King Percy are glaring at me with as much hatred as possible.

Turning, I look at Pierce and find Willow and Lydia smiling at me. My heart begins strumming, but I force open my mouth. "Please, take Elizabeth and K... Percy down to the dungeons."

Pierce bows and moves toward the new prisoners.

Both Percy and Elizabeth move back. They won't go down without a fight.

I don't want any more blood spilled. I connect to my power and create a fireball in my hand. I glare at them. "Please, don't make me use this. It'll be easier if you just cooperate."

Nick gasps.

Yes, I know. No one can control their powers like this. Only the Originals could.

Pierce grabs Elizabeth, and Jacob secures Percy. They haul them off as both royals glare at me with raw hatred.

Yeah, that's nothing new.

They are dragged out, and when the door shuts behind them, it echoes throughout the room.

Nick moves toward the middle of the room, his face lined with concern and his blue eyes on mine. "I am so sorry. If you want me to go to the dungeon with them, I'll go willingly."

Once again, a decision needs to be made by me. It's

stressful because these first ones are the most crucial ones I will ever make. I sigh and look for Owen, hoping to find some guidance. But as always, he's a blank slate.

I guess this one is all on me. I surprise myself with the fact that I don't want to punish him. Yes, he betrayed me and broke my heart, but had he not, I wouldn't have found Owen. Words that my mother spoke to me over a year ago filter through my mind. She was right. When his mother died, no one was there to protect him from his own father. He grew up a victim just like me, but he had no one to protect him or help him. I had Logan and my mother.

My heart thaws a little, and I take a deep breath. "No, you are a victim in this." I snort. "You're also my brother now."

He flinches and clenches his teeth.

Owen takes his place beside me and glares at Nick. He takes a menacing step toward him and clutches onto his shirt. "She has a tender spot for you, but I don't. I expect more going forward. If not, you will be joining your sister and father. Do you understand?"

Nick looks at the ground and nods.

Yeah, we have to work on his confidence.

Owen must have had the same thought, because he growls, "Look at me."

Obeying the command, he whips his head up to look at Owen. He gulps and nods. "Yes, I understand."

The door to the room opens, and Emerson comes through. She stumbles when she notices there are people in the room. Her gaze lands on me, and her eyes widen.

She bites her bottom lip. "What is going on in here, and where did you get that amazing crown?"

I'm not sure how to answer that. How can I explain it when I don't even understand what's happened myself? However, she needs to know since this impacts her. "Hey, want to go talk in the garden?"

Alarmed, Owen glances at me, but I ignore him. She's my sister, after all.

She gives me a puzzled look but nods.

I turn and give him a quick kiss on the cheek.

Taking my hand, he gazes into my eyes. *Are you sure she can be trusted?*

I glance back at her. She is rubbing her hands together and avoiding eye contact.

I glance back at him and give a small smile. *Yeah, I think so.*

He sighs, and it takes everything I have not to giggle.

I turn away and make my way to my sister.

Nick catches my eye and frowns.

I'm sure he isn't thrilled at the news I'm about to deliver. I keep my pace steady and nudge her. "Come on, let's go." I glance back at Owen. "Do you mind taking care of all of this?"

He looks directly at Nick and the Orlons. He responds in a deep, husky voice. "It would be my pleasure."

I'm sure it will be. I smirk and lead Emerson out the door.

Chapter Eight

The walk to the gardens is quiet. We can hear the sound of our footsteps echoing down the hallways, which are empty despite the time. I don't blame the people if they scurried home after the scene we all made tonight.

We approach the garden, and I miss a step. It seems as if it's browner, duller each time I come here. I begin walking again and make my way to my spot. I lean back on my favorite tree. "What is going on with nature? All the trees, plants, and grass are dying."

Emerson sits on the grass in front of me. She runs her hand over the browning ground. "Yes, it's been happening for a little over a year. However, it seems to have accelerated in pace the last few weeks."

I place my head against the back of the tree. I have very fond memories of this spot and don't want it ruined.

We both stay quiet for a little while.

Why am I postponing the inevitable? I just need to get

this out so I can get back to Owen. "A lot happened tonight."

She perks up, and I have her full attention. "Like what? I know something happened during the ball. And now, with that gorgeous crown on your head, there has to be more to the story."

I chuckle. "Yes, but more happened after." I push myself off the tree and attempt to sit beside her on the ground. Have I mentioned that I detest dresses?

Emerson turns her body toward me.

I rub my arms, trying to determine how to start. I guess, simple is best. She doesn't need to know the gory details. "King Percy was wrong. You're not the Savior."

She takes a sharp intake of breath. "What? How is that possible?"

I take a moment, needing to find the right words. "Because, I am the Savior. That's how I got this crown."

Her eyes flicker back to the top of my head, and she meets my gaze once more. "How is that possible? It's the second one ascending. I'm the second female."

I reach out and take her hand before I think that action through. Much to my surprise, she doesn't pull away. She threads her fingers with mine.

I squeeze her hand, attempting to be reassuring. "Logan has power, too."

Her body sags, and she leans forward, laughing.

Oh, great, she's about to have a meltdown. I'm not sure what to do. Does she think I'm lying? "Are you okay?"

She sits back up, and tears are running down her cheeks. She smiles at me. "I'm more than okay. Do you know what kind of burden this whole thing has been on me? I mean, I'm sorry it's fallen on you, but this means that I can finally breathe."

I was expecting a strong response, but this is not it. I can understand the strong sense of responsibility it places on someone, but she's had the burden since birth. I'm fortunate that it has fallen on me at the age of twenty.

Tensing, she stops laughing. "Oh, no, King Percy is going to be upset. I'm wed to Nick just because I am... was the Savior. What's he going to do to me?"

Despite being pampered her whole life, she realizes that her king has a bad temper. I pat her knee and pull my hand away. "Don't you worry about him. He is in the dungeon and won't get out any time soon."

Her face is in complete shock. "What? How is that possible?"

Laughing hard, I point to myself. "Being the Savior trumps the king."

She stays silent for a few minutes, running her hands through her long, dark, red hair. "That makes sense."

I rise, wanting to get back to Owen. "I hate to cut our time short, but I left a mess behind. Are you ready to head back?"

She gets up and we make our way back to the throne room. Right when we get back to the door, she pauses. "Everything is different now. What all is going to change?"

I wink at her. "Well, you're married to the Prince of Agrolon, and I'm the Savior. So, that means nothing really has changed except you aren't expected to save Knova."

A grin spreads across her face, and she flips her hair behind one shoulder. "Thanks, I needed that."

Opening the door, we both walk in.

The scene still looks very similar to how we left it when we went to the gardens. However, a huge table has been brought in and our group is sitting around it. They look up when we make our way in, and I notice that Jacob is on one side of Owen, but the spot on the other side, which is in the middle of the table, is left vacant.

Owen meets my gaze and winks. *Come take your seat by me.*

I continue walking, not breaking my stride, and take my seat beside him. On my other side is Pierce, then Lydia, and Willow. Directly in front of me is King Michael. His wife is in front of Pierce, and Sam is in front of Lydia, while Nick is in front of Owen. Emerson takes a seat next to her husband.

I glance around and hold my head high. That's what Saviors do, right? "What have I missed?"

Owen reaches for me and places our joined hands on the table where my wedding ring is right in view. He clears his throat and focuses on me. "The Orlons and Nick were informing us of the status of the West. Apparently, King Percy was holding back vital information."

That's not surprising. However, if we are talking motives and potential strategy, I need Logan. He's the only guard I can and am willing to trust. Dave's betrayal of being a spy for Elizabeth while training with my brother pops into my head. Not having to be on the front lines was worth keeping tabs on me. "Well, before we go into much detail, someone needs to fetch my brother."

Sam speaks up for the first time in a while. "Why do we need him? Everyone who is important is in this room."

Who the hell does he think he is? I scowl at him. "No,

you're wrong. He is more important to me than you are. So, no, not everyone of importance is in this room."

The corner of Owen's mouth is trying to curl upwards.

King Michael scowls at his son. "If Queen Ariah wants Logan in this room, well, that's how it will be."

I never expected to hear those types of words coming out of his mouth.

Standing, Pierce addresses the table. "I'll go get him. I'll be right back." He leaves on his mission.

I take in everyone. Nick is tapping his fingers on his chair, Emerson is staring at the table like it's the most riveting thing she's ever seen, King Michael is watching me, and Queen Lora is disgruntled. Sam's face is a little pink from the reprimand, and he's pouting. No wonder the West believes they can take over. We are just all over the place.

I glance down and notice that Willow and Lydia are writing notes back and forth, not wanting their words to be heard. I wonder what they are hiding?

The doors open and Logan appears.

Pierce closes the door behind him.

My brother's gaze lands on the table, and he pauses. He's dressed in his guard attire with his sword hanging by his side. His face is slack. "What are you doing?" He looks around the room. "Where is King Percy?"

I stand and point to the open seat beside me. "Please, take a seat next to me."

I glance at Pierce, hoping he understands why I asked Logan to take his original seat.

Nodding, he takes a seat next to Emerson.

Logan hesitates, giving me a strange look. After just a

moment, he makes his way over and sits beside me. He glances around the table and is tense in his seat.

I sit back in my seat and cut my eyes over at Sam. "Now that everyone is present, please, fill me in on the situation with the West."

Leaning toward me, King Michael places his elbows on the table. "Well, Crealon has been preparing for over a year. We thought it was imminent then, but they stayed put. Over this past month, they've been venturing out in the forest."

Something seems off. "How in Knova do you know this?"

Nick clears his throat and takes a deep breath. "Because we have someone on the inside."

What? How is that possible? "What do you mean?"

Slamming his hands down on the table, Logan looks furious, his green eyes wide. "Are you serious? That's Dave's special project?"

That makes no sense. "He spied on me so he wouldn't have to do fieldwork. How is he the inside man?"

My brother takes a deep breath and scratches his neck. "I thought you weren't so gullible anymore. Do you think Elizabeth kept her word?"

Wow. That hurt, but I deserved it. He's right. I've got to get my head in the game.

My husband turns and faces him head-on while looking at the Orlons as well. "I'm proud that my wife doesn't jump to negative conclusions. She's not gullible; she stands by her words and can't fathom why others wouldn't." He gestures to himself and the others around.

"That's why we are here, to help her see what she can't. Don't make her feel inadequate."

What? Does he believe that? I want to look down. I hate being the center of attention, but I force myself to stay steady and up.

Logan's gaze drops to the table. "You're right. I'm sorry."

Jacob shifts in his seat. "So, how far are they venturing? Do you have a timeline of when you expect them to attack?"

I'm so glad he is such a task-oriented strategist. All the attention is diverted off me.

Removing his elbows from the table, King Michael leans back in his chair. "We give it a couple of weeks, and then we expect them to venture farther. That's one reason why we were so relieved that Noslon made it here."

Sam huffs at this, and his father turns his head and glares.

Nick clears his throat. "Dave is expected to return tonight to provide an update."

Of course he is. Why don't we line up people that have hurt me at one time and just let me deal with it all in two days? "How was he able to spy?"

Nick rubs the back of his neck. "He gave them weapons to prove his loyalty."

Is he serious? They gave their enemies weapons? "Please, tell me you're joking."

Emerson barks out a laugh. "Why worry about that when the Savior is in your control?"

Oh, of course. Because that makes perfect sense. The arrogance of King Percy at his best.

The seat beside me pushes out, and Logan stands. "Is that where the weapons have been disappearing to?"

Did he take the weapons from the guards? How are they supposed to protect his people?

Nick rubs his hands down his face. "Yes, I know. But he is the king."

Smacking his palms on the table, Owen glares at him. "Just because he is king doesn't mean he's right. You are the future king of Agrolon. Why would you not fight for what's right? That's your duty to your kingdom and country."

Nick pales. "I've never thought of it like that before."

I reach out, touching Owen's hand. *Give him some slack. His father was cruel to him as well. He was raised to obey and fear him, not act like a leader.*

He cuts his eyes to me. *Fine. I'll lay off him for now.*

Jacob stands as well. "Can we go take inventory and see what weapons are missing? We need to know as much about them and what they possess as possible. What kind of weapons they have, what they received from Agrolon. The more information we have, the more of an advantage we can leverage."

They head to the weapons room, leaving the rest of us behind.

Rising from her chair, Queen Lora looks down at her husband and son. "I think it's been eventful enough for us today. Why don't we go rest and reconvene in the morning?"

King Michael stands, but Sam hesitates before joining them.

The king focuses on Owen and me. "I think it is best if

we retire. Can we meet up in the morning to discuss a game plan?"

I nod, thankful for their departure. I need time with my core group.

He bows, leading his wife and disgruntled son out of the room.

Lydia smiles at me. "My Savior and King, do you think it would be possible for you to meet me at the Pearson house first thing in the morning? I think there are some things you should know before making battle plans."

Yep, she knows something. I want to ask questions, but riddles will just get thrown around. So, I'll be patient for one more day. What're a few hours going to hurt anyway? I have a feeling, once I find out, I'll wish for my ignorance back.

Owen leans back in his seat. "Why can't you just tell us now?"

She tilts her head. "Because some information has to be told at the right time and in the best location."

There are the riddles. How fun. He isn't used to their ways like I am. "We will be there. We'll head that way after breakfast."

She smiles and turns to Willow. "Goodnight. See you soon." She walks out of the room without a backward glance.

I yawn and rub my eyes. This has been a long day, and bed sounds good.

Owen stands and takes my hand, pulling me up. He addresses the people left in the room. "Well, we've had enough for today. Let's meet up for lunch, and we can discuss next steps then since we will be tied up in the morning."

Nick nods, and Emerson smiles at me. Pierce bows before turning to leave.

Once we head out the door, Owen leads me toward the royal wing.

I stop in my tracks. "What are you doing?"

He smirks. "Taking you to bed, princess."

I glance back the way we had just come from. "Well, we are going the wrong direction." I point behind me. "It's back there."

He walks toward me, circling his arm around my waist and pulling me flush against him. His eyes are tender and his voice sultry. "If you think that I'm staying in your mother's quarters on our wedding night, you are mistaken."

His woodsy smell hits me, and his closeness makes my head spin. How did I get to be so lucky to have him as my soulmate?

He bends and captures my lips, making me forget where I am. He is in total control of the kiss, and I match his every move. My hands find their way into his hair, pulling him down harder against my mouth. He pushes me against the wall, and I moan in response.

Someone gasps.

Crap, we are acting inappropriately in the middle of a main hallway in the palace. I don't want to see who caught us. I don't think I can take anymore embarrassment.

Owen's chest is shaking with laughter.

I want to smack him. He's enjoying this too much. I

take a deep breath and look over his shoulder to find Emerson and Nick.

Smiling wide, Emerson winks, but Nick is not happy. His blonde hair is in disarray, and he has a huge frown on his face.

I move around Owen and stare at a spot on the wall. "Sorry, we got distracted."

She giggles. "I wish I got distracted like that."

Nick's cheeks turn red, and he glances down at the ground.

Wow, I guess their relationship isn't much of a marriage. I guess when your father is a controlling and manipulative man, it doesn't leave much for romance.

Owen turns and wraps his arm around me. "Well, I try to get distracted like that as much as possible."

I cringe. Did he just go there? I turn around and smack him on the arm. "My goodness, behave for once in your life."

He grins at me. "When it comes to you, I'll misbehave all you'll let me."

I cover my face with my hands, just wanting to disappear inside the wall. However, he's got that genuine smile on his face, and I love it when he misbehaves with me, so I can't complain too much. I chuckle and peck him on the lips.

Footsteps come down the hallway, and Mer comes into view. She arches an eyebrow and saunters over. She glances at Emerson and Nick. "Are they making you feel uncomfortable?"

Nick finds the ground again.

Laughing, Emerson glances my way. "No, it's fine."

Mer sighs and turns toward us. "People don't like watching you canoodle. It makes all of us feel uncomfortable. Get a room."

Owen lifts both hands up in surrender. "I was trying to, but she stopped me, telling me that I was going the wrong way. So, it's all her fault. Now, all of you guys scram so I can get distracted again."

"Oh, no, you don't." She grabs my arm, pulling me behind her. She turns to me and pouts. "Did you think Owen was going to stay at your mother's tonight?"

Are we talking about what's going to happen tonight in front of my sister and Nick? Does this family know no boundaries?

I open my mouth.

But she shushes me. "We have two quarters, and believe me when I say that Mother, Jacob, and I are staying in one and do not want to get anywhere near yours."

Oh my goodness, I want to die. I just wish she would be quiet and let me leave.

She winks at me. "Now, you guys go and have fun. I need to find Jacob." She walks off with a huge smile on her face.

I turn around and find Owen laughing. I point. "How many times do I have to tell you she has boundary issues?"

Nick grabs Emerson's hand. "Come on, let's... uh, leave these two alone for the night."

Chuckling, Emerson calls out behind her, "Have a good night. Enjoy being distracted."

This night is getting stranger by the second. What's

the oddest is that Emerson is laughing and joking with me. It is the strangest of all that's happened.

Owen scoops me up to carry me and smiles. "You know, your reactions encourage her."

I nod. "True, but she's so good at embarrassing me."

He kisses me on the nose. "I know, and don't ever change. It's the cutest thing."

I wiggle my feet. "Oh, by the way, I can walk, you know."

He continues walking, not missing a step. "True, but this is fun for me, and," he pauses at one of the doors and opens it, "I need to carry you across the threshold."

He puts me down on my feet, and I glance around. This room is beautiful. The walls are Agrolon yellow, and it has a floor plan similar to Mother's. However, this furniture is made of brown leather and the kitchen is huge.

We make our way into the large bedroom. The walls are that same yellow, and the furniture is made of dark wood. The floors are a lighter color that contrasts against the bed. The sheets are a cream color and the pillows are huge.

I walk over to the bed and plop down. He lays down, pulling me beside him.

We spend the rest of the night celebrating our marriage.

Chapter Nine

Ares is waiting at the stables for me, stomping his foot. I'm not sure how he knew I'd be coming, but he seems ready to go.

Owen shakes his head. "That stallion needs to learn some patience."

I cut my eyes over to him. "He's not the only one."

He reaches over and tickles me, grinning. "Take it back."

I can't control my laughter. "No, I won't."

Walking up behind us, Logan pauses. "Uh, hey, guys."

Owen lets me go but brushes my lips with his. He nods at my brother. "Hey." Then, he walks into the stables.

Ares walks over, nudging me.

Kicking at the ground, Logan watches me. "You heading somewhere?"

I pet the stallion and nod. "Yes, Lydia asked us to meet her at the Pearson house this morning."

JEN L. GREY

"Well, that's kind of strange." He glances back at the stables. "Do you mind if I come along?"

It seems like he should be coming with us. "You know what, I think that's a good idea."

"Okay, great. Let me get a horse." He heads to the stables, leaving me alone.

I lower my head down on Ares' nose. "We're about to learn a lot of information today, boy. I just hope we are all ready for it."

He neighs and stomps, ready to get a move on.

I laugh. At least one of us is eager. Ignorance is bliss most of the time, so I'm not in a hurry.

Owen and Logan come out with their horses in tow.

I mount Ares and wait for them. After just a few minutes, we are off toward the village.

His jade eyes shining, Owen comes up on my left side. "So, we caught a straggler on the way?"

"Yes." I glance at my brother and lower my voice. "I feel bad for him. I thought he could use a good influence."

Logan's forehead creases and he taps his finger on his lips. "Funny. I thought you guys could use a guard to protect you."

Placing his hand on his forehead, Owen looks up at the sky. "He has the same humor as you, princess."

I snort. He's right, though. Logan and I have similar senses of humor. At least he's kidding around with us again. Maybe things will calm down between all of us. "If he starts trying to kiss you, then we'll worry."

Owen chuckles and shakes his head.

"You just had to go there." Logan smiles at me.

The sun is rising, and I lean back, enjoying the

warmth. The path between the palace and village has always been one of my favorite rides. It's wide open, but the grass grows tall, giving it a prairie-like feel. I settle back on Ares and just enjoy the ride while I can.

Soon, the scent of bread and fish fill the air, indicating the village is just a short distance away.

Logan takes the lead, guiding us around the village instead of through town.

It brings back memories of my sleepovers at Claire's and training with Lydia. Even though those memories are good, I wouldn't want to go back to that point in my life. My whole life was in shambles and would only get worse. I'm so thankful for where I'm at in my life and with Owen by my side.

Claire's parents' house comes into view. "How are Grace and Derek?"

Logan glances back at me. "They're doing well. I help them out as much as I can, but they've been keeping up with the animals and crops."

Looking confused, Owen glances at my brother. "Are you saying that the village doesn't help them with their farming?"

Of course, this would confuse him. Back in Noslon, every person has an assigned job and contributes to the farming and hunting. "This is their farm, so they are responsible for it. No one helps them like back in our kingdom."

"But that doesn't make any sense."

How do I explain this? "This is how they feed their family and buy other supplies. It's a bartering system."

Logan scratches his head, messing up his hair. "How do things work in Noslon?"

"My father believed in taking care of his people." His tone is proud. "So, we all have community duties, and we share most of everything. For instance, we have a dining hall that cooks for the whole village."

Being back in Agrolon, it comes to light how each kingdom is run in a different manner. I just never thought of it.

We are silent for a while and turn down the path that leads us to the house.

Ares becomes excited and trots faster.

The Pearson house comes into view, and Lydia, Willow, and Pierce are standing out in the clearing in front.

I dismount from Ares and walk toward them.

Logan and Owen come beside me after a few moments.

Something seems off, but not in a threatening way. The energy just feels stronger than normal. And why are the three of them together? They are all from different kingdoms.

Willow grins, but her blue eyes seem uneasy. She walks over and gives her son a kiss on his cheek. However, when she makes her way to me, she takes my hand in hers. "I'm so proud to have you as a daughter. You are the perfect match for my son, and my loyalty lies with you."

What is she talking about? I glance over at Owen, but he has a bewildered expression. A lot of help he's going to be.

Staring at me, Lydia clears her throat. "I'm glad you brought your brother. It's time for you all to know the truth." She glances toward the house.

Owen glares at her. "Then please, continue."

Scowling, Willow scolds. "Be patient."

He cuts his eyes at her. "I've been very patient, more than I ever wanted to be, but only because my wife asked me to be. I want to know what we're up against, and the sooner, the better. I will not let her suffer because of your games."

Pierce nods. "I understand your frustration, but there were certain things that had to happen before we knew we could tell."

Clenching his jaw, Logan's tone is low and scary. "Like being thrown over a balcony or beaten by a king?"

Lydia nods. "Unfortunately, yes."

Nostrils flaring, Owen's mask of indifference descends on his face.

"Let me explain." She takes a deep breath and looks at me. "You never crossed my radar until you joined my class. I was foolish and took the king's word that Emerson was the Savior."

Wait, is she saying that she's known for a while that I am the Savior? "You knew that long ago?"

"No, but I became suspicious." She walks toward me, standing beside Willow. "Between your power being white and how the elements sought you out, I had to find a way to train you by yourself. And, for once, Elizabeth was helpful with something."

My mind flashes back to that day of training, where my power was uncontrollable and caused me to fall to my knees. Elizabeth pounced on the chance to belittle me. I chuckle. "Yes, she does like to insult me whenever she can."

She nods. "Between your strengthening powers, your pure soul, and how you took to training, I was almost convinced."

I tilt my head. "So, what convinced you?"

Her gaze lowers to my necklace where the key is attached. "Your key. That's when I knew the prophecy was truly beginning."

My eyes widen. "I never showed you the key. That's impossible."

She looks at me as if I were a child. "As I told you, I can see the color of one's power, and that key has power the same color as yours. You didn't have to show me. It caught my attention all on its own."

Who the hell does this lady think she is? "So, you let the king attempt to kill me, and let me believe that I would never see my family again?"

She arches an eyebrow, and her tone is harsh. "No, I didn't let that happen. I prevented you from dying and found you a way to escape." She holds her hands out in front of her. "You were still too weak and were not ready yet. You wouldn't have been able to stand up to the king. Your trials made you who you needed to be."

Taking her by the hand, Pierce pulls her behind him. He turns around to look at me. "You were unsure, child. She's right. You had to find your place in this world, but let me tell you that I'm honored I got to be part of your journey."

Even without a bond, I would be able to feel Owen's

anger pulsing off him. His gaze lands back on his mother. "Let's cut the crap. What was your role in this?"

She stands tall and glances at Pierce and back at Lydia. She takes a deep breath. "Lydia, Pierce, and I are Originals."

This should startle me, but it makes sense. They all seem to talk in riddles and knew more than what they'd tell you. However, I can feel my mate's betrayal and it breaks my heart.

He gasps. "That's impossible. They all died off long ago."

She smirks. "Yet, we're here."

I reach out and take his hand.

Squeezing my hand, he looks at Willow. "You didn't think that would be something I'd like to know?"

Sighing, she rubs her forehead. "Had I realized you were the Savior's soulmate, I might have done things differently, but my hands would have still been tied." She moves toward us, placing her hand on his shoulder. "I had no clue who she was or that you were her mate until she stumbled through our barrier that day. She was moving toward the cave, and I stopped her. When she dropped the key on the ground, I realized the significance."

I remember that day. She bent to pick it up, but it hurt her. That was the first time I ever saw Owen.

Tugging me toward him, his focus stays on his mother. "You didn't think you should tell me then?"

"All I knew was that she could be the Savior. I didn't realize you were soulmates until you forced that blood oath upon her." She points at me. "You were too busy trying to get her to leave. When did I have the opportunity?"

He growls. "Before she left the perimeter."

She glares at him. "I kept telling you that you made a mistake, but you didn't want to listen to me. You kept telling Mer I was going crazy." She takes a deep breath. "I couldn't come right out and tell you. You had some trials you had to conquer, too."

Logan crosses his arms. "Okay, we are losing focus. If you are all Originals, why were you in different kingdoms? Why did everyone believe you were dead?"

Those are good questions. Owen and I are too focused on people holding back information that we aren't looking at the big picture.

Sitting down on the ground, Pierce crosses his legs. "The longer we are together, the harder it is for us to go unnoticed. We had to separate."

"Wait? Are you saying you have powers, too?"

His honey-colored eyes meet mine. "Yes, but not like my sisters do."

What does that mean, and are they all related?

Owen leers at him. "Stop with the riddles and just tell us what we need to know. You're wasting time we could be using to strategize."

He nods. "That's fair." He runs his hand along the browning grass, almost as if in reverence. "I can shield myself and move fast and quiet."

So, that's why I didn't hear him that night I snuck out of the Orlon mansion. "And you acted like I was oblivious that night you caught me."

He smirks. "You weren't careful enough. You were too

desperate to let your power out. I helped you out that night with the guards or you would have been caught."

Owen glances at me. "What are you talking about?"

I let out a deep breath. "When I was at Orlon, I didn't use my powers for several days, and it became problematic. I had to sneak out one night to release it, because it was growing out of control."

Lifting her arms, Lydia looks disappointed. "What did I tell you about that?"

Is she being serious? I glare at her. "Yes, your lessons should have been at the forefront of my mind right after someone attempted to kill me and I had to leave my family behind."

Willow pats her on the shoulder. "She's right."

Wanting to get back on the topic at hand, I attempt to focus. "So, if you all split up so you wouldn't be detected, why are you back together now?"

"There are many reasons." Willow stares off into the forest. "One is that not all of us are together. The other is that, even though most of us are here, no one knows what our power feels like any longer, so no one is able to track us."

Owen holds his hands up. "What do you mean, all of you aren't together?"

"Yes." Pierce looks up at us from his spot on the ground. "We aren't. That's who is in the West."

Leaning back, Owen gets comfortable against a tree. "But we have an inside man. That's good."

Lydia laughs hard. "I wish that was the case." She looks up. "He's the one leading them and preparing them for battle."

Movement catches my attention in the Pearson house. It happens so fast, though, maybe I'm imagining things.

Owen frowns. "Why? What happened?"

Taking a deep breath, Pierce stretches out his legs. "He was always upset that he and I weren't like our sisters. He thinks it's ridiculous that we can't control the elements like them."

Logan's face creases in confusion. "But you guys can move fast and quiet. That's powerful in its own right."

"Not when you have someone who can blow you away or hold you in place by controlling the air." Pierce raises his eyebrow.

Glancing at me, Owen straightens. "What does he plan to do?"

Willow walks over to a tree and lifts her arm to touch it. "He's draining the elements instead of connecting and nourishing them. That's why all the plants are dying."

That can't be good. Or, at least, it doesn't sound that way. "Why would he do that?"

Lydia walks over and pats Willow's arm. "To have powers similar to us. He has become dark."

Of course he has. Something catches my eye again. I swear, there is someone in the Pearson house. "There is someone in the house."

Logan glances at me. "It's been vacant for generations. You're just imagining things."

Just then, someone is standing at the window, looking out at us.

I point. "No, they are right there."

Pushing off the tree, Owen looks over and glances

back. He takes my hand. "Are you okay? There isn't anyone there."

Grinning, Lydia laughs. "You are ready, my child."

What the hell is she talking about? I'm so tired of all these tests.

Logan scowls. "Explain yourself."

Motioning toward the house, she continues laughing. "She can see through the veil."

Owen looks back at the house and squints. "What are you talking about?"

Standing up, Pierce lets out a breath. "She can see Hazel even though we've put a barrier over it. Anyone who walks past sees an old, deserted house."

That's what happened that time with Logan. "So, if perhaps, someone saw a door slightly ajar and walked in, it would look like there were cobwebs and dust all over the place?"

Chuckling, Lydia points at me. "I thought you were going to figure it out then. You looked confused when you and your brother got outside."

Logan is confused. "What are you talking about?"

"Remember that day we came out here after your stitches were removed?"

He nods. "Yes, I do."

"We came here and the door was cracked open." My mind replays that day in my head. "We went in to investigate, but there were cobwebs and dust everywhere, so we hurried out. I thought my eyes were playing tricks on me, but once outside, it didn't appear that there was anything covering you anymore."

He holds out his hands, turning them over. "Why didn't you tell me?"

I shrug. "I had too much stuff going on at that time, so it was a fleeting thought."

Owen is staring at the house, almost like he's hoping, if he looks hard enough, she'll appear.

Willow's eyes brighten. "Let's try something" She looks at him. "Take Ariah's hand."

Turning to me, Owen winks. "I don't have to be told twice."

I giggle. He has a way of making me feel special. I hope that never changes.

He intertwines our fingers and brushes his lips against my cheek.

"Okay." She bounces on the tips of her toes. "Merge your powers and see if you can make out Hazel."

I push my power out toward him, and his responds. Times like this, I don't know where I begin and he ends. We are connected in such a way that we feel like the same person. I can hear his thoughts and him mine.

He wraps his arm around my waist and opens his eyes. "Yes, I can see her."

All of a sudden, a small portion of my power reaches out beyond him. What the hell is going on? Once it reaches Logan, it stops and surrounds him.

Logan gasps. "I can see her, too. How is that possible?"

Willow's mouth drops open. "Am I seeing things?"

Shaking her head no, Lydia pales.

Pierce walks toward my brother, his face pale. "Your power is surrounding him, and it appears to be sharing it with him." He glances at me. "Pull back and see what happens."

I ask the powers to come back to me, and they flow back and merge with my mate.

Logan rubs his eyes. "I can't see her anymore. What the hell?"

The door of the Pearson house opens, and Hazel sticks her head out. "I think I figured something out Instead of just staring at me through the window, why don't you all come in?"

Putting her hands on her hip, Lydia juts out her chin. "Well, we didn't realize you were asking for us to come in. But why can't you come join us out here?"

Hazel's eyes glow with her power. "Because the portal is in here."

Dropping her hands to her side, Lydia bounces on the bottoms of her feet. "Well, why didn't you just say so? Yes, let's join you." She heads toward the house.

Willow comes over and rubs my arm. "Come on, we need you for this." She looks at her son. "I promise it's okay. I wouldn't risk either one of you."

I glance back at my brother, who is still a little shell-shocked from earlier. He hasn't moved from the spot.

Chuckling, Pierce glances at him. "You'll be okay, too."

Huffing, Logan stays still. "I'm not worried about my safety, but if I go in there, will I even be able to see what's going on?"

"Ahhh…" Willow shakes her head. "Yes, I'll make sure you can." She walks over and pulls a piece of hair out of his head.

"Ouch." Logan's tone is harsh. "What the hell was

that for?"

She narrows her eyes at him. "Do you want to be able to see what's going on in there or just the veil?"

He rubs the top of his head where she pulled out the hair. "Yes, but a little warning would have been nice."

She heads off and works her magic on the barrier.

I can tell it has worked, because Logan's eyes brighten, and he moves ahead of us to walk inside the house.

We walk into the house, and my suspicions are confirmed. The interior is immaculate, clean as if someone is living here. The kitchen takes up half of the main living space, with a round table in the middle that can easily seat eight. The appliances are older, and instead of having an electric stove, there is a wood-burning stove centered on the far wall. Despite that, it's clean and has running water, and the rest of the house looks modern enough.

The living room is connected, so you can't tell where one room begins and one ends except for the kitchen table. There is a nice couch in front of the fireplace, and a bookshelf against a wall that is filled with ancient-looking, leather-bound books. There is a hallway that appears to branch out to three bedrooms and a bathroom.

The inside of the house is trimmed in wood, but the walls have a fresh coat of paint, making them a natural, light brown. This feels like home.

Making her way in front of the fireplace, Hazel is bouncing with excitement. "I found a way."

Lydia chuckles, walking toward her. "Of course you did."

I hate how they do this. "Found a way to what?"

Pierce stands beside me in the kitchen. "A way to quickly get to Crealon. She made a portal somewhere. That knowledge had been lost, but it's a task she has focused on for the past year."

Standing on my other side, Owen looks around me to see him. "You're Originals. How was the knowledge lost?"

Willow touches his shoulder, and he cringes.

Hurt crosses her face. "We may be Originals, but portal generation was never common knowledge amongst our kind. The leaders didn't want anyone abusing and taking advantage of it, so when our kind was attacked, the ones who housed that knowledge were killed."

I guess every society has their rules. At least, Hazel figured it out and it can help us with Crealon.

Logan sits at the kitchen table and plops his feet on top, making himself comfortable.

Who does he think he is? "What are you doing?"

He shrugs. "Making myself comfortable. I figure we will be here a while."

Glaring, Lydia stares at him. "Please, remove your nasty feet from my table."

"You all are living here?" He puts his feet back on the ground. "I don't think you asked permission from us."

Hazel tilts her head. "No one lived here for years, and it was neglected to the point of falling apart until we tended it. No permission needed to be asked, for the door was open."

I close my eyes. She makes my head hurt. Can't she talk to us like a normal person?

Willow moans and her eyes glow. "We need to go. There is something going on at the palace."

Chapter Ten

The room goes silent until Logan rises from the table to walk out the door.

I grab Owen's hand and pull him outside, where we catch up to Logan.

His face is set, and his focus remains in front of him. He doesn't slow down. "We have to get back. Claire and Mother need us if something is going down."

He's right about that, but I'm not as worried. "Yes, we do, but Mer and Jacob are there. They'll take care of them."

Logan cuts his eyes over at me. "That might bring you comfort, but I don't know them." He points at himself. "It should be me protecting them." He takes off in a run.

Owen tugs my arm. "I would be the same way if it were you. We'll catch up."

I glance behind us to find Pierce and Willow are following close behind. "Are Lydia and Hazel not coming?"

Nodding, Pierce catches up. "Yes, they are. They won't be far behind us."

I turn back and focus on making it back. When we make it to the horses, Logan is already gone. I hope nothing happens to him on the way.

Owen points to the horses. "I'll ride with Ariah, and the two of you can ride the other."

Shaking his head, Pierce walks past the animals. "No need for me. I only ride them to keep up with appearances. I'll be fine by foot."

Without a pause, Willow mounts the other horse, while Owen and I get on Ares. Of course, he slides in behind me.

Within minutes, we are making our way back to the palace. Pierce takes off and disappears from sight.

The ride back is in complete silence. I don't know what to expect, but something has to be off considering Willow's reaction. "What's going on at the palace?"

She takes a deep breath. "I don't know. I could feel panic but couldn't see what was going on. I just know we need to get back."

Well, that's helpful. It would be nice to know what we are walking into.

Owen leans forward. "Don't worry. It will be okay."

It's crazy, but I believe his words. He has a way about him, and he doesn't promise what he can't deliver. I hope this isn't the first time he's wrong.

The palace comes into view, and nothing looks out of sorts. That should comfort me, but it puts me on edge.

We run through the gates and I dismount off Ares. Owen and Willow hurry into the stables to put the animals up and are back beside me within minutes. When they reappear, we are cut off by Pierce.

He glances our way. "We need to hurry. I'll meet you down in the dungeon." Then, he disappears again.

Looking around, Owen searches for him. "Damn, he does move fast. He just disappeared."

Willow ignores him and looks at me. "Where are they?"

I wait a second as memories of the dungeon come crashing through my mind. The king liked to beat us down there amongst all the criminals. The last time I was down there, I came home with blood pouring down my back and onto my legs.

Owen takes a sharply inhaled breath. "He did that to you?"

He can always read my mind at the most inopportune times. "Now's not the time to discuss this." I look at her. "Follow me."

Leading the way, I walk through the main palace doors. I push open the white wooden doors, and they slam against the walls, the sound echoing. Rushing past the main stairway, I turn down the hallway that leads to the dungeon. The hallway is narrow and feels claustrophobic, but it's the only way downstairs.

When I get to the end of the hallway, there is a stone door and the lights are low. I pull at the door, but it doesn't budge.

Owen reaches around me. "Here, let me try." He pulls at the door.

"It's locked." Willow looks at me. "You can unlock it with your power."

Yes, if I can control the wind, I should be able to use it to unlock the door. I just need to focus. I pull him out of the way and bend so I'm at eye level with the keyhole.

She walks beside me and turns her hand over so her palm is facing up, and fire burns, lighting up the area. I see where the lock is and push my power toward it asking the air to turn the internal mechanism. When it responds, an audible click indicates it worked.

Owen grabs me by the waist and opens the door, going through it first.

Of course he would, but now is not the time to complain.

We walk down the stairs, Willow following me. When we get to the bottom, it's so quiet that not even the inmates are making noises.

Pierce materializes from what appears to be thin air.

I almost squeal but stop myself before the sound lets out. I scowl at him and talk in a soft tone. "Do not ever do that again."

He bows his head and looks over at Owen and Willow. "We need to hurry. Marcus is here."

"Marcus?" Who the hell is that?

She blinks. "Our brother."

Wait. The one causing this mess is here? How does no one but us seem to know?

Pierce turns and motions for us to follow him.

When we get farther in, we find that all the inmates are unconscious and lying on the ground. What the hell?

We come across a cell that has the door wide open. We approach the door and find Dave sitting in the cell, tied up in a chair.

Serves the jerk right.

A deep laugh comes from behind us.

I spin around to find a dark-haired, olive-skinned man with deep, soulless eyes. He's tall but smells of decay.

He smirks and scans me over. "You're not what I expected." He points at Dave. "He said you were very beautiful, but he still underrated your beauty."

Owen walks beside me and wraps his arm around me. "She's taken, so back off."

Marcus lets out a grating laugh that sounds like nails on a chalkboard. His gaze stays on me, and he rubs his chin. "Well, you better get going."

Wait. Did he just say we better get going?

Owen takes a step toward him. "Okay, I'll bite. Where are King Percy and Princess Elizabeth, and why should we get going and not you?"

Yes, let's take a step toward the menacing-looking man. *What the hell are you doing? Stop antagonizing him.*

Marcus smiles, his teeth yellow. "King Percy and I have come to an agreement of sorts, and because my whole army is here, but we came in peace if you're willing to not fight us."

Looking around, Pierce lifts his chin. "Bring them out. I will fight you."

Marcus sneers. "Do you think it will be that easy?"

Oh, no. He's been planning this for a while and is already many steps ahead of us. What are we missing?

Frowning, Willow's eyes glisten with unshed tears. "Why are you doing this? We are family. We can still be one. You don't have to do this."

His body stiffens and quivers with rage. "Don't you

dare. It was you who came up with this grand plan. Let's all split up and blend in. Why should we blend in when I can rule all of Knova?"

"But you can't without sacrificing the very thing we're supposed to protect." She holds her hand out toward him. "Don't do something you cannot undo."

"Who told us we had to protect it?" He glares at her.

She takes in a short breath. "That's our destiny. It is what we were trained for."

"We were always told that, but they were wrong." He raises his arms out and closes his eyes. "We were meant to lead."

She looks defeated.

Moving next to her, Pierce rubs her shoulder.

Marcus lowers his arms, and his eyes find me once again. "Come join me, and we can rule together."

Stiffening with contained rage, Owen's power is stirring.

I meet the crazy man's gaze. "No, I'll pass."

He purses his lips into a kind of one-sided smirk. "Then you better get going."

I shake my head. "I'm not going anywhere."

"Yes, you are." He lowers his head. The air begins churning around me.

My power flares in response.

He chuckles. "You aren't ready for me. It's kind of a pity."

The air lifts me off the ground. Owen is struggling to get to me, but something is holding him back.

The air feels thick, almost suffocating. Much to my horror, I'm moving closer to Marcus.

Willow and Pierce struggle to get to me as well, but even they aren't able to fight against his power.

He's grinning, and the closer I get to him, the more I can see the deep lines in his face.

I've got to do something. I close my eyes and picture a knife cutting through the air around me. It seems crazy, but that seems to be what I need to do. The air around me wobbles, and I fall to the ground.

I land on my feet, and right now, I'm not going to overthink that part.

His eyes widen, and his hands light up with red flames. He throws it at me.

I call my power up and shield myself.

Owen reaches out and connects to the water in the air. He pushes the water toward Marcus, catching him off guard.

He looks at Owen. "How is that possible? You are a male."

I push my fire toward him, letting it nick his skin.

Appearing right before him, Pierce punches him in the mouth.

Nostrils flaring, Marcus clenches his fists. He moves his arm and has Pierce slammed against a wall. "Enough. I've humored you way too long."

He closes his eyes and, with a groan, wipes the blood away that is dribbling from his lip.

The room changes. I can feel the elements as they are sucked toward him like he's draining their life force. The walls rattle and crack from the force. He's going to collapse the whole area.

I try to move, but I'm stuck in place.

His eyes open, and I'm slammed against the wall hard.

My head throbs from where it hit, and my vision wavers.

Marcus roars. "This is your last chance. Leave now or die. I want a worthy adversary, so everyone knows that I defied the prophecy. If you don't go, my knights will attack the village."

Being released from whatever hold was on him, Owen runs over to me, panic clear on his face. "Are you okay?"

I can't move. *Just a little rattled.*

He scoops me up and carries me out of the dungeon.

What the hell is he doing? We can't leave the village to him. Much to my chagrin, Pierce and Willow are following behind him.

Marcus's laughter rings in my ears. *What the hell, Owen? Turn around. We can't let him win.*

Ignoring me, Owen picks up the pace.

Willow shouts behind us, "Go to Ariah's mother's quarters. That's where we need to go."

He turns and the familiar path comes into view.

My head is now spinning so I close my eyes.

The door is open when we get there, and several different voices filter out of the room.

I want to see what's going on, but the pain has intensified.

Lydia is here, busy instructing the group. "Thank goodness you guys are here. This is bad, but move to the center. Willow is going to transport us out here. Marcus is hoping to follow us and see where we go."

Moving to the center, Owen holds me tighter.

"What the hell happened to her?" Logan's tone is rough.

"Now is not the time, for we have lots to do." Hazel's voice comes closer to me. "Huddle close. Ears are everywhere."

Is it bad that, even in immense pain, Hazel gets on my nerves?

She mutters under her breath, and the room seems to waver. The air seems to vibrate against my skin, and it feels as if I'm being stretched from head to toe. It's intense but disappears as fast as it came. There are several gasps, but I have no clue who it all belongs to.

Holding me close, Owen kisses my cheek and takes off.

I sure hope he knows where he's going. A door opens, and the smell of home hits me. *Are we back in Noslon?*

He lays me down on our couch. "Yes, and we need to heal you."

Someone else rushes into the room and moves to sit beside me. I flutter my eyelids and find Mother, Logan, Willow, and Claire there.

Willow walks toward us. "Please, move back. We need to take care of her."

Glaring, my brother stays put. "That's what we are trying to do."

She touches his shoulder. "Please, trust us."

Taking his hand, Claire pulls him away with her.

Owen sits beside me and presses his forehead against mine.

I coax my energy toward the location of my injuries

and connect with him. However, I somehow connect with someone else in the room as well.

Disentangling himself from Claire, Logan moves toward the couch, coming on the other side of Owen. He touches my arm.

How the hell am I connecting with him, too?

Laying his forehead on mine, Owen's breath blows across my face. "Just focus."

He's right. I'm about to lose consciousness.

Connecting with both of them has me healed within minutes. I pull my power back inside me and open my eyes.

Logan's body tenses and he sits straight up.

Pecking me on the forehead, Owen runs his fingers down my cheek. "Don't push it, okay?"

I love that man so much. I rise and find Claire puzzled.

My mother takes a quick step in my direction, her face white. "What are you doing? Lay back down."

I grin at her. "I'm fine."

She covers her mouth. "Are you saying you healed yourself?"

Okay, why is this a big deal? "Uh… yes."

Claire gasps. "Only one Original was ever able to do that."

Why don't I know these things? "Yeah, but when it comes to healing myself, I need Owen's help. Logan helped the process go faster."

Mother blinks. "How is that possible?"

I look at Owen. *Do we tell them?*

He nods.

Yeah, I guess it is time. "Owen and I are soulmates."

Walking over and sitting down beside my brother, Claire leans into me. "How do you know this?"

I show her my wrist, and Owen places his wrist next to mine.

Mother sits next to me on the couch and looks over. "Oh, my goodness. How is this possible?"

Like I have an answer for her. "I don't know, but the fates must know what they are doing. Or, at least, I like to hope they do."

Reaching out, Mother traces the tattoo on my wrist. "The thorns mimic the key. This is unbelievable. This is a big deal."

You're telling me. "I know and I wouldn't have it any other way."

She glances at Logan. "But how are you involved?"

The time for family secrets is over. Too much has happened. "Well, Logan and I have been bonded for many years."

Dropping her hands in her lap, she looks at my brother and me. "I always thought something was different between you two. Why didn't you tell me?"

Logan lets out a breath. "Really? Is that a serious question?"

Placing her hand on her chest, she stands up from the couch. "What does that even mean? Yes, it's serious."

Claire stares at me for a minute. "It was for our protection."

I smile. She knows me so well.

"Yes, but I have a right to know what's going on with my children." She takes a few steps and refuses to meet my eyes. "I should have been there for you." She walks out the door.

I stand to follow.

But Willow steps in front of me, blocking my way. "Let me talk to her. She needs some space." She winks at me.

I want to disagree, but she's right. We have more important things to worry about. I sigh and nod. She turns and heads out the door.

When the door clicks, I turn back and sit on the couch. "All right, who all came with us?"

Owen shakes his head. "No clue. I was too worried about you." He tugs me closer to him. "You have got to stop scaring me like that."

I snicker. "I promise, it's not on purpose."

Standing, Logan plops down on the couch between Owen and me. He wiggles in until he's pushed me a good distance away.

Claire laughs, and even Owen is trying to hide a smile.

My brother looks at him. "That's my sister. I get it, but don't want to see it."

I snap my fingers, trying not to grin. "Focus. Who is here?"

Leaning back, Claire raises her hand. "The whole crew." She lifts a finger one by one as she names our party. "The Orlons, Nick, Emerson, Gabe, Lydia, Hazel, Mer, Jacob, and everyone that was here."

Did she say Gabe? "Father is here?"

Logan chuckles. "Yup, apparently, he wants to speak to you."

Of course he does. I stand and make my way past the couch. "All right, well, let's go make plans."

Owen grabs my arm. "Why don't you rest for another minute? I mean, you were hurt pretty badly."

I peck his cheek. "I'm fine. Marcus is taking over Agrolon. There is no time to waste. We need a plan."

He opens his mouth, but I turn and walk out the door.

As I leave to make my way toward the lake, I realize the three of them are just standing and not following. "Why aren't you coming?"

Owen raises an eyebrow. "Princess, they are in there." He points to the dining hall.

Okay, I knew that. I walk past them.

Claire is snorting. I tap into my power and blow some dirt their way, because that's what real ladies do.

"What the hell?" My brother is trying to contain his laughter.

Feeling accomplished, I head into the dining hall.

This time, they follow.

Mer attacks me when she sees me enter the room. She's hugging me so tight that I am struggling to breathe.

Jacob appears and pulls her off me.

She crosses her arms. "Why'd you do that?"

"Because she was injured not even twenty minutes ago."

She points a finger at him. "That may be the case, but she isn't now. I can touch my sister if I want to." She winks at me. "I can say that now that you're tied to my brother."

I chuckle. "I wouldn't call it tied."

Owen wraps his arm around my waist. "Nope, definitely not tied."

She leans on one foot. "Yet, that's exactly how I see it."

I laugh and head to the table. It's so strange to see everyone here. Emerson, Nick, and the Orlons are in their fancy clothes. It is so out of place from this natural-looking setting. And even though Agrolon had a huge, fancy dining hall, the servants served them. While here, everyone goes through the food line and sits at the exact same tables. There isn't a special table just for Owen and me. We are all equals.

Emerson, Nick, and Gabe are on one side, while Queen Lora sits in front of Emerson, King Michael across from Nick, and Sam is sitting in front of Father.

Father appears to be in shock. "How are you healed? Just a few minutes ago, you were in bad shape."

I didn't think this part through. They want answers. "Perks of being the Savior." I sit next to Emerson. "Is everyone okay?"

Sitting down beside the Queen of Orlon, Mer takes a huge bite of her venison. "Yeah, you were the one who got your ass kicked. I guess you aren't at Savior level yet."

King Michael sits up tall. "How dare you talk to her that way."

"No, it's fine." I put my hand on the table. "She just speaks the truth."

Owen sits beside me and puts a plate of food in front of me. "That may be the case, but she doesn't have to be so rude." He hands me a fork. "Eat or I will make you. You need your energy."

I want to argue, but he's right. My stomach is growling. I take a quick bite, but unlike Mer, I chew and swallow before speaking. "So, what happened?"

Clearing his throat, Jacob begins. "I failed, that's what

happened. I was distracted and didn't notice that there was a commotion at the front gates." He sets down his fork. "I found some guards passed out by the palace entrance in the back and realized that something was amiss. Mer and I hurried to make sure your family was protected."

How were they distracted? Jacob looks uncomfortable, so I don't want to press it now. I'll ask later.

Mer motions toward the Orlons. "I went to grab Emerson, and everyone else here now followed us." She looks at me. "Not my fault. I tried to leave them behind."

I bite my lip to keep from reacting. That's one of the things I love most about her. You know where you stand.

Queen Lora glares at her. "Yes, why is that? We've been loyal and upfront."

Shifting in his seat, Jacob's body is coiled. "Yes, now. After you discovered that she," he points to me, "is the Savior. Before then, you and your son wrote her off."

King Michael gets up. "That's enough. You can't talk to us like that."

Standing up to mirror the other king's actions, Owen's mask of indifference slips back into place. "Actually, he can. We like frank conversations here. If you can't handle it, then you are welcome to leave."

Nick's eyes land on mine. His blonde hair is in disarray, and there are dark circles under his blue eyes. "They're right. We all wrote Ari off. We are lucky to be here and should be thanking them instead of trying to wave our status around."

Sam stares at the table but nods. "They are right. We aren't worthy to be here."

Well, at least those two have the sense to look ashamed. They were two of the people I had trusted most of all. "The past is the past. Let's keep it there, but right now, we need to work together. We can't allow our kingdoms to be overrun."

Frowning, King Michael crosses his arms. "How do we know we are any safer here?"

Owen's jaw twitches. "Because we have a barrier here. It will be more difficult for Marcus to find. We are hidden. That's what took you all so long to find us. Had Jacob and I not been out hunting that day, your guards may still be looking."

Relaxing at the comment, he sits back down to finish eating. Owen follows suit, and the table descends into silence.

It feels so weird having them here. I glance up and catch Emerson's eye. She smiles at me and seems to be enjoying herself.

That's so strange. Her whole demeanor has changed ever since she found out that I'm the Savior. Maybe she should have been. I didn't do too well tonight.

Once I finish my meal, I glance over at Owen. "Let's go to the lake, away from prying ears. I don't want to worry the others right now."

He nods and stands. When we head toward the door, Mer and Jacob follow close behind us while the rest of them look around, not sure what to do. They are so used to servants, they don't know how to clean up after themselves.

Looking back, Mer stops in her tracks. "Are they serious?" She walks back over to the table. "You see this?" She points to the trays. "You take them over to the garbage cans and dump the scraps. It's called cleaning up after yourself."

Sam just stares at her with his mouth gaping open.

Queen Lora's nostrils flare. "Is this some kind of joke?"

Grabbing the tray, Mer holds it out to her. "Nope, not at all. We all pull our weight around here. You're no better than anyone else."

Running interference, Sam walks over and takes the tray from her. "Don't worry, Mother. I'll take care of this."

Mer shrugs and heads back over to me. "Yeah, she and I aren't going to get along."

"Just remember, she's always lived a privileged life. She doesn't know anything different."

Mer opens her mouth, but I hold a finger up. "I'm not saying it's right. Just give her time to adapt and cut her a little slack."

Brushing his lips over mine, Owen cups my cheek. "You are too kind, but I love that about you. You put things in a different perspective for us."

Soon, Gabe makes his way over. He stops a few feet away from us, which makes the whole situation even more awkward.

I take a deep breath. "Father, have you met my husband?"

He clears his throat. "Not really." He holds his hand out.

Owen hesitates before shaking his hand, making the situation even tenser.

Emerson walks up and pulls me into a hug. "I was so worried about you. You looked like death ran over."

I hug her back. "I'm sure it won't be the last time someone tries killing me. We are at war."

Scratching the back of his neck, Owen looks at me. "This isn't something to joke about."

Gabe stays silent.

Mer tilts her head. "Isn't that something a father should agree with?"

"Of course I agree with it." He sighs. "I just don't know if I've earned the privilege to speak up."

Wow, did he really just admit that? I don't have the energy to analyze this right now.

The rest of the group make their way over, and we head out. When we reach the lake, we find Mother and Willow sitting on the embankment.

I'm about to turn around and just relocate, maybe cram our group in the house, but Mother turns toward me.

She gets up and envelops me in a hug. "I'm so sorry. I didn't mean to be ugly; it's just that it's my job to protect you. I should have pushed or just known, but I get why you didn't tell me."

Stepping beside us, Logan joins in on the embrace.

She shakes her head. "You both have tried protecting me all this time. I guess that's what families do."

Owen puts his hand on my back. *Your sister feels left out.*

I hadn't thought of that. It's just been the three of us for so long that including Emerson in this moment didn't cross my mind, but she is family, too. I pull away and hold my arm out to her. "You belong in here, too."

Mother's face brightens. "Yes, I can't remember the last

time I got to be close to all three of my children at one time. Please."

She hesitates for a minute but then hurries to us. Mother deepens the embrace, pulling us all closer.

Of course, Father stands back next to Nick.

I detangle myself from the group hug. "We have things to discuss."

Owen turns to the others. "What happened while we were gone?"

Stepping forward, Nick is the first to speak up. "Nothing was amiss until I noticed the guards were missing."

King Michael nods. "Yes, we were at breakfast when we noticed something strange was going on. We headed back to the royal chambers." He motions toward Jacob and Mer that are standing to the side. "That's when your friends came along."

Mer places her hand on her hip. "I'm their sister."

It so typical for Mer to be lost on that fact and not the severity of the problem. "Okay, now that we have that established…" I glance back at Nick and King Michael. "Did the staff seem strange?"

Stepping beside his father, Sam shrugs. "No, they were attending to their business as usual."

My father focuses on me. "What happened to you all?"

I glance at Owen. I was unconscious for almost half the time, and I'm not sure how much we should share.

Owen takes his place beside me. "We were visiting with Lydia at the Pearson house as requested. When we arrived back at the palace, there was something off."

Something was off, all right. Willow's crazy moaning didn't help.

Owen must hear my thoughts, because the corners of his mouth twitch. "We wanted to go talk to Percy and Elizabeth, so we headed down to the dungeon."

Did he just call King Percy by his common name? Fatigue begins creeping in, and I have a hard time concentrating. I daze off as Owen brings the rest of our group up to speed.

The thing that keeps repeating in my mind is how much stronger Marcus is than me. How are we supposed to defeat him?

Gabe rubs his chin. "How did you get out?"

Pierce walks out of the woods behind us. "Because he let us. He wants to beat Ariah fair and square when she's at the height of her powers." He looks at me. "He knew she wasn't there yet. He wants to say he defeated fate."

Mother sighs. "Haven't we dealt with enough unbalanced people by now?"

"So, it appears my father and sister have aligned with him." Nick walks over to a tree and leans against it.

Crap, I hadn't really thought of that. He's right. This is even more of a mess.

Looking off, Sam taps his foot. "How did this guy know where to find them?"

Logan barks out a laugh. "Let me guess. Dave?"

I snap my fingers and point at him. "We have a winner."

"Serves that boy right to be tied up like he was." Willow shakes her head in disgust.

I lean against Owen. It's late afternoon, but I'm

exhausted. He was right. I should have taken it easy, but I won't admit that to him.

Tightening his hold, he glances down at me. "Ariah needs rest. We will meet up in the morning and work out a plan."

I want to argue but don't have it in me. I nod my head and lay it on his shoulder.

Owen pauses for just a moment. "Jacob, will you please show them to their houses while they are here?"

He nods. "Yes, sure can."

We move back and walk past everyone.

My eyes droop. "I'm so tired."

"Well, you almost died today. That probably has something to do it with it." He opens the door to our house and scoops me up in his arms.

My lids lower. "I can make it up the stairs just fine."

He chuckles and then I'm out.

Chapter Eleven

Waking up in my own bed is one of the nicest things in Knova. I didn't realize how much this place has become home to me until I went back to Agrolon. I won't leave again. They are all stuck with me.

Owen walks into the room and sits on the bed. "You're finally up."

Huh? "What do you mean?"

He points at the clock. "It's lunchtime."

I sit up. "Why didn't you wake me? We need to talk strategy."

He rubs my arms. "Calm down. We met this morning and discussed things. You needed your sleep."

The front door opens, and I lay back down. "One, two, three."

"Time to wake up." Mer is stomping through the house, banging around.

I pull my hair. "Will she ever learn her boundaries?"

Owen's shoulders shake with laughter.

Her footsteps are now echoing up the stairs. She's coming, and there is no escaping.

The sound stops at the door. "You guys are dressed, right? I'm not going to walk in on something, am I? There are just some things that can't be unseen."

What did I ever do without her? Before I can even tell her to come on in, she is already opening the door.

She peeks through the crack. "Oh, good. You're decent."

Owen turns his body toward the door. "What would you do if we hadn't been? You just walked right on in."

She walks in and sits on the bed with us. "Well, one, I didn't hear any noises, so that was encouraging."

Did she just go there? I don't think she understands boundaries at all.

Tilting her head, Mer leans toward me. "Look at her. Now a married woman and she still blushes." She shrugs. "Anyways, two, you had just walked over here, so I thought, if something was going down, I would interrupt before the show got started."

He glances at me. "You're right. She has always pushed, but she's gotten out of control. We'll change the locks tomorrow."

She gasps. "You wouldn't."

Crossing his arms, he nods. "Yes, it's time. We're married now and need some level of privacy."

I throw the covers off me. "Okay, enough of this. Where is everyone?"

She stands. "They are eating, but being the loving

sister I am, I brought you some lunch over. It's downstairs in the kitchen."

Looking at me, Owen cringes. "I asked her to bring lunch. That's why I didn't complain when she just came in. Her just waltzing into our bedroom is a whole different story."

I stand and walk to the door. "I'm starving."

I lead the way downstairs and find one of my favorite meals, venison stew. I sit at the table and eat it as fast as possible. I want to get with the others and figure out what's going on.

Owen joins me. "This morning, we met and discussed strategy. We need to focus on training together. Marcus is too strong. We're missing something. The others agreed and plan on helping around Noslon and training to fight until we're ready."

Whoa. The royals are going to train to fight? That's interesting. "What about Emerson? She's strong, too, even if she isn't the Savior."

"Speaking of which." Owen glances out the window. "Mother is going to be here in a second, along with your family. We have some things we want to discuss away from the others."

"What about?"

Mer plops into the seat next to me. "We have no clue. You know how she is."

I laugh. That's true. I finish up my meal and go upstairs to change into some regular clothes. When I enter the room, I notice the wooden box laying on my bed. "What the hell?"

Walking over to it, I open it, and sure enough, there is the crown inside. I pull it out and hold it in my hands. I rub my fingers over the two empty places like something used to belong there. The Agrolon yellow jewel is in one divot, and a Noslon black rock in the second. The other two appear as if whatever was in it has fallen out. What could it be?

There are voices downstairs. Crap, I need to hurry. I change and head downstairs with the crown in hand.

Willow notices me first. "Where did that come from? You left that back in Agrolon."

"Apparently not." I take a spot on the couch beside Owen.

Emerson is sitting at the kitchen table with Claire and Logan. Mother comes over and sits on the other side of me, and my father steps through the door and stands beside Willow.

Why the hell is he here? "What are you doing here?"

Reaching out and patting my leg, Mother scowls at me. "Be nice. He's your father."

"I realize this, but he's never cared to be around before."

He frowns and looks down at the ground. "I deserve that."

Sighing, Mother looks disappointed, but I ignore her. It's strange, him being here.

"All right," Willow claps. "So, after yesterday, I think I've figured out the three and the key."

Now, she has Owen's attention. He turns his gaze to her. "Okay, so what is it?"

She glances at Emerson. "Do you often know things about Ariah that don't make sense?"

Looking down at the table, she answers in a soft tone. "Well, every time I was drawn to the garden, she was there. Also, I didn't believe she was dead, because it seemed like I could feel her inside me."

"Don't encourage this." Gabe looks up. "This is crazy talk."

Willow ignores him. "Logan, we've established you have a bond with Ariah, and Owen does, too." She looks at me, her eyes shining. "She's the key. You three are bonded to her, and she is the key for you all."

Taking a step back, Gabe frowns. "Are you saying the Savior is the key."

Mother bites her lips. "Well, when you explain it that way, it makes sense."

Does it make sense? I don't feel a bond with my sister, and Logan's is faint compared to what it used to be. "I don't feel her, and I don't feel Logan like I used to."

"That's because you weren't close to your sister, so you didn't understand. We need to practice your connection. And with Logan, as well." She sits on the coffee table in front of me. "As you got stronger, you couldn t feel him, but his intensified. You are the link to them all."

She glances down at the crown and a grin spreads across her face. "Wait, I know what that needs." She runs out the door without another look.

Mer motions toward the door. "And you say I have problems."

Claire snorts. "I love you."

I can't focus on them around me. Is what she saying true? I glance at Emerson, and her eyes lock with mine. Do we have a bond?

A familiar sensation takes over my body. So, when I realize I'm floating in the air, I'm not worried. I glance down and, sure enough, my body is sitting up staring at the door. Why do all these strange things happen to me?

"What is going on?" Emerson is right beside me, floating as well.

She can do this, too? "You get used to it."

Emerson startles and looks my way. "You're up here, too? What do you mean, you get used to it?"

"It's happened to me several times now. I don't know how to control it."

She chuckles. "Well, I was just wishing we could talk alone."

Huh, maybe that's it. "What did you want to talk about?"

"Well," she begins, moving a little closer. "Is it bad that these past few days have been the best in my entire life? I hate that this burden got put on you, but even if I'm part of the three, I'm not the Savior. I can be myself for a change."

I smile. "No, I understand. I'm glad you're happy. I didn't know who I was either, but for different reasons. It took me a long time until I did, and I'm still figuring out the small details."

The door opens, and Willow comes back in. She takes the first step and looks right up at us. "Please, get back into your bodies. We need to talk."

What the hell? She can see us? These Originals are sneaky. How in Knova do I return to my own body? "Do you know how to get back?"

"This is my first time." She taps her lip with her fingers. "Maybe we just swoop down?"

"Wait, when I use my power, I push it out." I close my eyes. "Maybe we just need to push toward our bodies."

I envision myself floating down. When I blink, I'm back.

Owen is staring at me. "What was that?" He grabs my hand.

"I have no clue, but at least I figured out how to get back to my body whenever that happens." I look up to where I was just a few seconds ago. "Every other time, I had to wait until I went back on my own."

Mer pouts. "Why can't I do that?"

"Oh, no." I point at her. "You already have boundary issues. I don't want to imagine what you would do or see if you could do that."

Moving a few steps back, Gabe is making his way toward the back of the room. At the palace, he was always in the middle of things, so it's odd to see him on the outskirts.

Willow pulls something out of her pocket. "Here, let me see the crown."

I hold it out to her, and she pulls out an emerald jewel. My jaw drops. "Wait, isn't that from the ring?"

She grins. "I told you I would know when it would be needed."

The jewel fits perfectly into one of the divots in the crown, clicking into place. The emerald from the engagement ring Sam gave me is the jewel that fits in the crown.

Owen glances at the jewel and at me. "What ring?"

Yeah, this won't go over well. "Sam gave me a ring right before I left Orlon."

His jaw tenses and his body stiffens. "What kind of ring? Why would he give you a ring with a jewel?"

Mer's tone is soft but loud. "This is about to get interesting."

Getting up, Claire walks over to her. "Maybe we should tone down our excitement."

Wrapping an arm around her, Mer winks. "Don't worry, the princess can kick her husband's ass."

Claire mashes her lips together, trying not to laugh. "I'm not worried about her. I'm worried about the one who gave her the engagement ring."

Now, I wish I'd never brought it up.

His face hardens. "You were engaged?"

I reach out to him. "No, no. He proposed, but I said no."

"Then why did you have that ring?" His power is thrumming with his rage.

I don't want to lie, because that would be the easy way out. I take a deep breath. "Because he wanted me to have it for when I changed my mind."

Owen gets up and marches out the door, not looking back.

Standing, Logan claps. "I hope that prince gets what he deserves."

Okay, so Owen and Logan are good now. That's nice, but I need to get to my irrational mate fast.

Claire's forehead creases. "I don't understand. What's the big deal? She said no."

Taking my hand, Willow leads me to the door. "They

are soulmates. That's different. They are connected and possessive. He takes it as a challenge."

We are hurrying and head to where the hunters are. I guess this is where the men are training. When we walk up, Jacob is standing in between Owen and Sam.

Sam's hair is wild, and he is wearing Noslon clothing.

His father is right beside him and still in his royal garbs.

Holding both hands out, Jacob is keeping the two apart. "I don't know what's going on, but you need to calm down."

Growling, Owen leers at him. "I'm your king. Do not tell me what to do."

Sam snarls. "Let him through. I'll take him."

Shrugging, Jacob looks back at Sam. "You asked for it." Then he moves out of the way.

Clenching his fists, Owen shoves Sam in the chest, making him stumble a few steps back. "She is mine."

"Only because she thought I was going to turn her away." Sam steps forward, refusing to back down

Emerson and the others catch up.

Walking between them, Emerson points at Sam. "You, shut up." She turns to Owen. "And you, be rational. She is your wife, and this all happened before you. Don't throw the king card around if you aren't going to act like one. Look where it got Percy."

Snorting, Mer pats Owen on the back. "She got you there, brother."

I join them and place my arms around Owen. "Overreacting much?"

He glowers at Sam. "Still not happy he gave you that ring, but at least it's not in that form any longer."

I frown at the Orlon Prince. "I never said yes to marrying you, and you know things wouldn't have worked out. You were about to kick me out, so let's not act like you're the wounded one here." I snuggle into Owen's side. "This is my husband and the one protecting you right now. Act grateful and play your role. It's time for you to grow up."

Grinning, Jacob looks at me. "If we are done here, I have some training to do."

Owen nods and we head back to the house.

Mer calls out to us, "I'm going to stay here and help."

On the way back, Gabe comes up beside us. "Are you really bonded mates?"

I don't want to talk to him. He has never made an attempt to get to know me until now. "Yes, we are."

He rubs his forehead. "How do you know?"

Owen glares at him. "We have matching tattoos that occurred at the same time."

Joining us, Mother smiles. "Yes, they are beautiful. I'm sure you'll get to see them sometime."

When we reach our house, we all pause outside.

Willow walks up. "My bonded family, do you mind if we all go train? This is a crucial step to winning against Marcus."

I glance around. "Let's do this."

"I won't be any help." Mother takes a step toward the lake. "Aren't there some medicinal fields I can help tend to?"

"Yes." Owen smiles. "There are. If you go past the

dining hall and keep on the path, you'll run into them. They are hard to miss."

"Okay, I'll do that then. I'll see you all at dinner." She turns and heads that direction.

Gabe watches her walk off. "I think I'll join her. Good luck training."

I hope he doesn't hurt her, but right now, training is more important.

Chapter Twelve

We arrive at the normal field that Owen and I use for training.

Willow takes her usual spot and leans against her favorite tree.

It breaks my heart, because all of the trees are almost solid brown, and now, we know why. It's all Marcus.

Emerson's eyes soften. "It's so sad. The trees are dying."

Nodding, Willow motions to the dying plants. "That's why we have to focus on this training." She looks at me. "You are the key, so you are the link to each of them. Let's start with you connecting to them, and then we need to make it so they can connect to you if needed."

Okay. Simple, right? I decide to connect to Owen first. He's the easiest for me. I push my power out to him, and we sync with one another as soon as we merge. It's strange, because, with him, our connection is all-encompassing. I can't tell where he begins and I end. We are intermingled.

I turn my attention to my brother. I open our bond in my mind and let my connection run into him. When I do this, I can tell what he's thinking and feeling, but I can tell the difference between his thoughts and mine. There is a line of my power connecting us.

Once that happens, I turn to Emerson. How in Knova do I connect with her?

Owen steps to me. *Try surrounding her?*

It's worth a shot. So, I imagine my power spreading out and surrounding her body. When that happens, I can sense her. But it's not the same as with the others. I can't tell her thoughts or feelings, but I can sense what she's smelling, hearing, and what's around her.

Willow's eyes are wide and her mouth is dropped open.

When I look around, our power is lighting up the entire place. It's swirling around us all and thrums through us.

Watching us, Lydia steps into the field. "Sorry, I'm late, but it looks like I got here right in time."

She has her typical, large bag over her shoulder. She pulls out a target and hammer, then walks over to the tree right beside Willow and hammers the target on the middle of the tree. "I want you to make a fireball and hit the target."

How the hell does she expect us to do that? "We are supposed to hit only the target?"

Lydia crosses her arms. "No, I expect you to hit the target. You are the key and the one who can do it."

Oh, great. No pressure at all. I try to calm the thrumming of power coursing through me. It's almost overwhelming, like it used to be right after I had reached Enlightenment. Lydia helped me then, so I'm confident she can help me now.

Instead of pushing the power out like I used to, I force it into my whole body, letting it fill up everywhere. It courses under my skin, but it's not uncomfortable. I focus on the target and push the power out toward it.

Willow pushes off the tree she's leaning on and ducks down.

The fireball hits where she was just standing, leaving a gaping hole in the center.

Well, that went great. Not only did I miss the target, I almost killed my mother-in-law.

Owen chuckles beside me. "It's okay. It was an accident." He winks. "Right?"

Helping Willow up, Lydia glances my way. "Well, that did not go according to plan."

Coming over, my brother puts his hand on my shoulder. "Hey, she tried. Are you okay?"

I nod. "Yes, the power wasn't overwhelming after I pushed it throughout me, but it's too much for me to handle."

"Well, that's what we need to focus on." Willow looks back at the tree. "If you can do that, once you get the power under control, you'll be unstoppable."

Yes, it's always about me getting control. It's so frustrating. "Again."

Lydia smiles. "That's my girl."

Taking my hand, Owen squeezes it. "You can do this."

Yes, I can. The problem is that I need to learn fast. The longer I'm training, the stronger Marcus is getting. "All right, let's do this."

Our power is still connected, so I focus, distributing it so it's not so overwhelming. I push the power out and it hits the top of the tree where the target is.

Emerson grins. "You got closer."

Never expected her to be an optimist. "Yes, but I didn't hit it."

Watching me, Willow holds up a hand. "I think we should be done."

"No, I'm good." I look back at the target. "Let me try again." I push my power toward it, and it hits right on the edge of the target.

Owen grins. "Good job."

I smile but begin to wobble on my feet.

Logan and Owen both grab an arm and help steady me.

I release my connection to them, too tired to maintain it.

Concerned, Willow comes over and pats my cheek. "I could tell you were about to tire out. Your eyes dimmed. You need to go home and rest. We will try again in the morning."

I hate that she's right, but I'm exhausted. Connecting to them and trying to contain the power did take its toll on me.

Lydia picks up her bags. "You did well. The same theory as a year ago applies today. The more you drain yourself, the more resilient you will become. Go rest and be ready for tomorrow."

Owen leads us back to the village, and we pass by Claire in the square.

She runs over to me. "Are you okay?"

Taking her hand, Logan pulls her away, letting me have some space. "Yes, she's just worn out. We had a good training session."

We walk into the house, and I plop down on the couch.

Owen grabs a drink and brings it to me. "Here, you need to drink this. It'll help a little."

I take it from him and take a large sip.

He sits on the other end of the couch and pulls my feet into his lap. "You don't need to push yourself so hard."

I glare. "Yes, I do. We have someone we need to put in their place."

Emerson walks over and takes my empty cup. "You were great. I couldn't have done that. I can't believe you're my sister."

No, I'm not great. I learned that at a young age.

"She is great." Claire stares at me. "She just needs to realize that."

My brother sits at the table and groans. "She's cocky enough. Let's not encourage that."

I crack up. "Thanks for keeping me humble."

Owen takes my shoes off and rubs my feet. My energy is springing back to life.

Well, I sure wasn't awesome today. What did I do wrong? I've got to get this under control. The longer we take to train, the more Marcus is able to destroy.

We sit in silence for a little while when there is a knock at the door.

Logan opens it up and finds Nick standing there. Emerson's eyes light up when she sees him but dim again when he remains standing near the door.

He leans back against the wall, dressed in solid black. "How was training today?"

I lean back further against the couch. "Not great."

Owen pats my leg. "She did spectacular, especially while being tapped into three different people at the same time."

"Not good enough." I sit up. "Is it dinner time?"

Nodding, Nick smashes his lips together. "Yes, that's why I am here. I was coming to see if you all were ready for dinner."

I put my shoes back on and head to the door.

Claire comes up next to me, and Emerson walks over to Nick.

We follow them out the door, and they are not standing close at all. They aren't talking and are more than a few feet apart.

They've been married for over a year, so it's strange to see how distant they are with each other. I had hoped they would have grown close, despite the forced marriage.

Logan and Owen are behind us, talking about strategy. I'm glad they are getting along. I guess, since we're all bonded to each other, we have to play nice.

Claire touches my arm. "This place is amazing, and you appear to be at home."

I run my fingers through my hair. "Yes, this is my home. Agrolon never felt that way, but this sure does."

"I'm glad." She glances at the darkening sky, the sun setting. "You deserve to be happy. I'm so glad you found

Owen. He completes you and makes you stronger. You've come a long way."

Arms wrap around me, and I lean back into Owen. It's hard to believe we haven't known each other my whole life.

Nick opens the door and stops to wait for us to walk in. Keeping her eyes on the ground, Emerson looks miserable. I don't know how to make things better.

We walk in, make our plates, and head toward the table where the Orlons and Originals are sitting.

Of course, Mer and Jacob are sitting there, too. They've combined four tables together to fit everyone.

I walk over and sit next to Willow. The Orlons are on the end and the Originals in the center.

"How are you doing?" Willow gives me a hug.

"I'm okay." I pick up my fork. "Just a little tired and very hungry."

Emerson walks over and sits next to Lydia, and Nick sits across from me.

Setting her plate down next to his, she watches him.

He ignores her and smiles at Lydia and me.

Lydia takes a bite of her food. "Ariah, you did well. Don't get discouraged."

Sliding in next to me, Owen looks around me at her. "She won't listen to you. She's been pouting all afternoon."

That traitor. "I have not."

Logan plops down his tray next to Owen. "Oh, yes, you have. It's been written on your face the whole night."

"I have been contemplating ways to improve."

Emerson tilts her head. "Is there a difference?"

What the hell? Her, too? "When did you get so talkative?"

She looks down at her plate. "I didn't mean to be rude."

"No." Crap, I feel bad. "I didn't mean it like that, either." I forget how careful I need to word things with some of the Agrolon natives.

Hazel is talking as she eats.

This causes Mer to give her a dirty look. She leans around them and looks at me. "Is this normal for people where you come from?"

Jacob groans.

She turns to him. "What's your problem?"

He takes a sip of water. "You say I have no manners, yet you go and say something like that?"

She puts her elbows on the table and glares. "It's an educational question."

Willow lets out a deep breath. "No, this is just Hazel. She connects to the elements in a different way than most. Just leave her be."

"Hey, where are Mother and Father?" I look around. "They aren't here."

Lydia bites her lip. "I ran into them, and they said they wouldn't be around tonight. They had some plans."

That's strange. What are they up to?

After we are done eating, Jacob hands a piece of paper to Owen. "Here are some of the training techniques I was thinking of teaching them, but I would love to go over them with you and get your opinion."

I get up, needing to be alone, and this seems like the perfect opportunity.

Owen grabs my hand. "Can this wait until the morning?"

"No, it's okay." I kiss his cheek. "I'll go down to the water and rest. I'll meet you back home in an hour."

His jade eyes stare into mine for a moment, but he nods. "Okay, one hour. I'll see you then."

I leave before he changes his mind. I love him, and being around him is great, but there are times when I need to think on my own. I walk down to the water and sit on the embankment.

It's strange to have my family here, but it also seems to fit. However, I can't keep Marcus out of my head. I have to learn how to get a handle on this power.

Also, what do King Percy and Princess Elizabeth know that could aid Marcus when it comes to us? There are so many uncertainties.

Did fate make a mistake by placing me as the Savior? I always wondered what if, but now, I'm wondering if Emerson would have made a better one than me. Why has the fate of our country fallen on my shoulders? The girl who grew up worthless?

Someone sits beside me, and I'm alarmed until I realize it's Pierce. "You scared me."

He smirks. "I shouldn't have. Marcus can do this and more. We need to get you acclimated to my powers."

I nudge him with my shoulder. "I should have known your cat-like reflexes were not ordinary."

He chuckles. "Don't be too hard on yourself. You're learning."

I lean back on the grass. "Yes, but I don't have time to learn. I need to know."

"But you've grown so much in a short amount of time." He leans back next to me. "You'll get this quickly, and it gives us time to train Nick, Sam, and Michael for battle."

Wait, did he say Michael? "You're not calling him King Michael?"

"No." He stares out into the woods. "In battle, formalities cannot be made. We are all equals and on the same team. We have one captain, that is the best warrior, making the calls."

I snort. "I bet he loves that."

"Believe it or not, he hasn't had a problem with it."

That is surprising. "Well, that's good. Maybe I built him up to be something different than he is."

"Just remember." He turns toward me. "Trust your gut. Your powers will let you know what needs to be done. Believe in yourself and things will get better."

Someone clears their throat behind us, and I turn to find Owen there.

He crosses his arms. "Sorry, I'm worried about you. I couldn't be away that long."

I get up and wrap my arm around his waist. "No, I'm glad you're here."

Pierce takes off toward the forest. "Good night. I will see you all in the morning."

Owen grabs my hand, and we turn to head home. "Let's get you home and let you rest. Tomorrow is a big day."

Chapter Thirteen

☙❧

The next few weeks fly by. Every day, the four of us train in the field with the two sisters, and the king and princes train with Jacob.

As we walk into the dining hall for breakfast, I sit beside Mer. "Good morning."

She glances at me and leans toward my ear. "So, I think Sam and Emerson have a thing going."

What? "No way, she's married to Nick."

"I found them last night in the barn together."

"That makes no sense." I can't believe what she's saying.

She laughs. "Just watch."

Owen and Jacob come over and join us, so that cuts the conversation short.

Owen raises an eyebrow at me, and I shrug.

Smiling, Jacob turns to him. "I'm surprised at how well Nick, Sam, and Michael are doing. They are almost as good as seasoned fighters, especially Nick."

Owen nods. "That's good. We need all the reinforce-ments we can get."

He's right. I've gotten better, but I'm not where I need to be and the forest is already almost dead. We're running out of time, and we all know it.

The Orlons come in and join us at the table, with Claire and Logan right behind them.

Glancing at me, Claire sits down. "We came by your place last night and knocked on the door, but you guys didn't answer. Were you not at home?"

Mer chuckles. "No, they were probably busy, if you know what I mean."

Queen Lora tsks. "A lady shouldn't speak that way."

Oh, this isn't good. This won't go over well.

Scowling, Mer turns all her attention to the queen. "Well, here, we say what we mean and pull our weight, unlike some guests who take advantage of our grace-fulness."

I glance at Owen, but it's futile. We all know she is just speaking the truth. Even King Michael went to training and is trying to help the kingdom, but his wife is not.

All of us at the table are dressed in Noslon clothing, except the queen. She has refused to change outfits and insists on rewashing her royal garments each day. She stays at the house provided until it's time to eat, but then is negative when she does open her mouth.

"I am a queen, so I have different standards." She pats her mouth with a napkin.

Pointing at me, Mer glares at her. "So is Ariah, but she's training every day."

She's dragging me into this. Great.

Holding her head high, Lora sticks her nose in the air. "Yes, but she was brought up differently."

Mer's nostrils flare.

Glancing at Lora, Claire picks up her fork. "So, in other words, you can't handle any physical pressure."

Mer bursts out laughing.

However, Lora's face turns to stone. She puts down the napkin. "I can handle any kind of pressure."

The queen just got baited. It amazes me at how observant Claire is.

"Then I challenge you to some physical training with the men." Mer takes her last bite of food.

Michael scratches the back of his neck. "I don't think that's wise, and how are you going to train wearing those clothes?"

"Don't worry." Mer stands up. "I'll go find her some appropriate clothing right now."

Taking another bite of food, Lora nods. "That's fine. Let's meet back at my guesthouse in thirty minutes."

Walking out the door, Mer leaves on a mission.

I glance at Claire, who gives me a small wink before going back to eating.

Don't ever underestimate her.

෴

WHEN WE ARRIVE AT THE TRAINING SITE, LYDIA, HAZEL, and Willow are already there. They are standing by the large tree that is beginning to sag. All the trees are this way, but the largest one is sagging the most.

Hazel walks over to us. "There is no more time to

spare, for death is coming. The trees and flowers feel it, and we will all feel it, too, if the Savior doesn't master the key."

Yes, I get it. I have to figure this out. "Got it."

She nods and goes back to her place beside the tree.

Reminding me that he is there, Owen rubs my shoulder. *I love you. You've got this.*

I connect with the three of them like that first day, and I focus on the target. Even though I can hit it, I can't combine the elements without it causing a huge problem. Last time, when I tried to use water to put out a fireball, I wound up lighting a small portion of the forest on fire. That's not good for anyone.

I push the fire toward the arrow, but unlike all the other times, instead of pushing the water toward the fire as well, I pushed it toward Owen. *You send the water to the fireball.*

He doesn't hesitate and does what I ask. It works.

Willow looks at him. "You used your power for water. How is that possible when you were all linked?"

Smiling, Lydia looks at me. "That's it. You're the key, which means you can decide who uses what power. That makes sense. You don't have to be the one controlling it all."

We practice a while longer, but at this point, we all have it. Logan and Emerson are able to know what I'm asking them to do because of our connection. Even though they can't hear me like Owen, they understand my intent.

Excited that we've figured it out, we head back. When

we walk back to our kingdom's barrier, Pierce appears and his whole body is tense.

Logan steps forward. "What's wrong?"

Glancing back at the village, Pierce flinches. "He's been here."

Owen growls with impatience. "What do you mean?"

"Marcus. He left Ariah a gift on the other side of the barrier."

"He's found us." Willow looks at us. "We knew we couldn't hide forever."

"What did he leave?" Lydia crosses her arms.

Emerson's face pales.

My brother is resolved. "At least we figured a large part of it out."

Pulling me near, Owen's jaw clenches. "Where is Jacob?"

"Back at the hunter's ground." Pierce motions behind him.

Owen moves toward them. "We need a strategy."

We all head toward the hunters and find Jacob, the Orlons, Nick, and Mer there.

Sporting a busted lip, Mer has a deep scratch down her arm.

Dressed in all black, Queen Lora has a swollen eye.

I almost don't recognize her. They really did fight.

Jacob and Nick are standing near the barrier, looking at something on the ground.

Owen, Logan, and I walk over.

There on the ground is a small box and a piece of paper that is folded in half that says 'For Ariah'. "What the hell?" I bend down to get it.

Grabbing my arm, Owen is scanning the perimeter. "No, he could be anywhere."

Emerson moves our way. "What is it?"

Blocking her path, Sam steps in front of her. "No, you don't."

Crap, Mer wasn't kidding when she said they've been getting close. I need to talk to her.

Glaring, Emerson moves around him to stand beside me.

Our group is hovered close to each other, looking at the box, but not one person is doing anything about it.

I reach for my power and lift the box to bring it inside the barrier.

Mer snorts. "That's one way of doing it."

Owen reaches for the box, and I grab the letter.

Ariah,

It seems you are mastering your skills. I hate that you rejected my offer, so I thought it would be best if I left you with a gift.

Oh, and tell Claire her parents say hi.

See you soon,

Marcus

I snatch the box from him and open it, not really wanting to know what's inside. When I see a knotted lock of blonde hair, I forget to breathe. Oh, no, please don't tell me this is Claire's mother's hair.

My hands tremble and my stomach rolls. He has Claire's parents.

Owen reaches out to steady me, but Logan and Claire move next to me before I come to my senses.

"What's going on?" Logan focuses on me.

Claire looks down and sees the hair and reads the note. Her eyes widen. "What does this mean?"

Confusion is all over Logan's face until he reads the note. "Oh, this isn't good."

"What does it mean?" Claire's tone is loud and frantic.

Owen and Jacob look at each other. Feeling my heartbreak, Owen turns his attention back to me.

Grace is like a mother to me.

He tilts my head up. "It means it's time for war."

Mer whoops. "I've been waiting for this. I can't wait to kick some butt." She walks over and puts her arm around Lora. "My friend and I are ready."

Wait... "You guys are friends now?"

She nods. "Yeah, she put up a damn good fight."

"Yes, and I realized how impractical those clothes are for combat." Queen Lora frowns in disappointment.

There are some things I won't ever understand, and this is going to be one of them. "All right, let's go to the house and makes some plans. All hands on deck."

I glance at Jacob. "Can you go find my mother? I swear, I haven't seen her in weeks."

He gives me a thumbs-up. "On it. I'll meet you all at your place."

Where has she been? She's disappeared as well as my father.

Claire is crying.

I don't know how to help her. We have to get to her parents, and soon. Marcus has made it clear that they are at risk.

We make it back to the house, and the Orlons sit at my kitchen table along with Nick and Emerson.

Emerson's face is white, and she keeps tapping her feet.

Nick has buffed up while he has been here. His blonde hair is cut shorter, and his face is tanned. From what Jacob is saying, he's turned into an awesome warrior. It's as if he's taken his abuse and channeled it into his training.

Another prince seeming to do well is Sam. The only problem is that he tends to not focus at times and expects others to protect him. However, he's toned up and seems willing to help.

King Michael has stepped up and been training hard. He's focused on saving his people, and despite everything, I admire that of him.

Mer plops down on the couch next to Claire. "Don't worry. We're going to get your parents back."

This causes Claire to cry harder and bury herself further in Logan's arms.

Owen comes up behind me and rubs my shoulder. "Don't worry, princess. We'll get them."

I turn around and snuggle into his arms. Even though it's been a while since I've seen Derek and Grace, they are still important to me. Why didn't I consider the fact that Marcus could get to them?

The front door opens, and Jacob walks in with Mother and Father behind them. Much to my chagrin, they are holding hands and smiling like they don't have a care in the world.

She stops short when she notices Claire. "What's wrong?"

The door opens, and the four Originals come through.

Mer glares at my mother. "Maybe you'd know if you weren't too busy reconnecting with your husband and ignoring everything else. Even Ariah and Owen never ditched us like that, and they are soulmates."

"Listen here." Gabe's glaring at her. "You can't talk to her that way."

Mother puts her hand on his arm. "No, she's right. I got carried away. I'm so sorry." She glances back at Claire and looks at me. "What's going on?"

Rubbing my shoulders, Owen looks at my mother. "Marcus has Claire's parents. He left Ariah a note."

Gabe cringes. "It's King Percy. He told him."

Staring at me, Hazel walks to the center of the room. "The time is now. You must overcome or Knova will be gone."

She makes her way to Nick. "Be sure to hit the center or things won't be as you know."

Queen Lora leans her head back against the chair. "Please, just be quiet. No one can make sense of your riddles."

I take a deep breath. "Okay, enough. Let's not fight. We have to figure something out. It's time to fight. Knova is dying, including the medicinal fields. It's gone on too long. Now, we need to determine a plan. We can't go in blind."

"Yes." Owen takes my hand. "He's going to be watching us, so we need to figure out the best way to go in while making the least bit of noise."

Lydia smirks. "Well, that's easy. Hazel can get us to the Pearson house easily. We can just channel there."

Jacob rubs his chin. "That could work, but wouldn't he

have been suspicious when he didn't see us leave last time?"

"No, he was cocky. He was letting us leave." Pierce paces. "However, even if he was suspicious, he wouldn't know where we would enter."

Running his fingers through Claire's hair, Logan pulls her closer. "So, we could teleport to the Pearson house. That's close to Claire's parents' house. There is no telling where he is keeping them."

Owen's body tenses. "You're right. He may not have them at the palace. That's probably the best bet. We can check out their house first on the way."

Either way we go, we're going to have to face him. I guess, going to their house first and not the palace, where all the guards will be, would be ideal.

Claire sits up and wipes her eyes. "We have to go get them. They could be hurt."

Sighing, Sam crosses his arms. "I guess that's the plan. We are going in, ready or not, to save some parents."

"Yes, we are." Emerson's tone is commanding.

"All right, let's get a good night's sleep and meet at the dining hall for breakfast. There is no telling when we will be able to get a good night's rest again, so sleep up." I take a breath, taking in each person. "This will be the end of the war."

Chapter Fourteen

When the last person walks out the door, Owen turns to me. "Are you sure about this?"

I sit on the couch. "Yes, Claire's parents took me in and were kind to me when I was at my lowest point. I can't turn my back on them."

Owen plops on the couch beside me and grabs my leg. "All right, I get it." He leans back on the couch and looks at the ceiling. "I just don't feel like we are prepared. That's a big deal, since you're going to be the main target."

I lean against him. "I know, but you're never going to feel like we're ready, are you?"

He puts his arm around me and pulls me closer. "No, you aren't worth the risk."

I snuggle closer. "It's coming, no matter what."

He puts his chin on my head. "I'm worried. He knows you are getting stronger, and he knows where we live. I'm afraid he's pushing you before we've had time to train thoroughly to ensure he can beat you."

He's right, but it doesn't matter. I can't do that to Claire. "I get it, but it doesn't change anything."

"Come on, let's go to bed." He gets up and heads toward the stairs.

I follow behind him, and we spend a little time together before calling it a night.

⚜

OWEN IS SOUND ASLEEP, BUT I JUST CAN'T REST MY WEARY mind. After tossing and turning for a while, I decide a trip down to the water might do me some good.

I crawl out of bed, trying not to disturb him. He needs all the rest he can get. I make it downstairs without bothering him and go out the front door.

When I reach the water, Emerson and Sam are sitting on the embankment way too close to one another. I almost turn around and head back home, but this has to stop. She's a married woman and a princess no less. "What are you guys doing out here?"

Emerson startles and turns to face me. Her cheeks are so red that it's noticeable even in the darkness.

Looking at the forest, Sam refuses to meet my gaze.

Mer was right. Something is going on between them.

She scoots away from him. "Oh, I just came out to get some fresh air and stumbled upon Sam."

"Well, good thing I'm here to keep you company." I cross my arms, daring Sam.

Sam holds up his hands. "Nothing has happened. I wouldn't do that to her."

Startling, Emerson sucks in a breath. "What does that mean?"

Okay, that's good. She's in a loveless marriage, but she's still married. "It means he respects you, which is good. Still, if anyone else had stumbled upon this, it wouldn't look good."

He looks behind me. "You're right, but we started out as friends. Since arriving here at Noslon, my feelings began to change."

Emerson takes his hand. "What do you mean?"

He bites his lip. "It means I've fallen in love with you."

She looks so happy.

This isn't good or appropriate right now. "You're married. You can't do this without getting a bad reputation."

Her shoulders sag. "I know, but I'm not happy."

I figured that. She and Nick don't even speak to each other unless necessary. "I'm sorry, but we have to figure this out and handle it the right way. You promised on Knova."

She wipes at her eyes. "That's when I thought I was the Savior and was told that it was best for us all."

My heart breaks for her. She's not the only one who was forced into things for the sake of the prophecy.

Owen comes into the clearing. The corner of his mouth is twitching. "I come out here and find you with him?"

I glare at him and turn back to Sam. "Can I have a minute with my sister?"

He glances at the ground and nods. "Yeah, I can give you that." He meets my gaze. "I'm not trying to cause problems, but I really do love her."

I reach out and touch his shoulder. "I get it, but you can't go sneaking out at night and meeting her in random places."

He chuckles. "I did with you."

Owen takes in a sharp breath, and his power thrums.

I don't need this right now. Sam just confessed to being in love with Emerson. "Yes, but I wasn't wed. This is a whole different situation."

He turns toward Emerson. "She's right. We shouldn't be so careless. Goodnight, everyone. I'll see you in the morning."

As soon as he is out of sight, Owen smirks. "I'm so glad I came."

"You were asleep." I put my hand on my hip.

He comes over and kisses my lips. "Well, you getting upset woke me. I thought I should come check on you."

I didn't think about that. *Hey, I need to talk to Emerson alone. Be back in a few minutes?*

He takes a second and stares into my eyes, then pulls away. "All right, I'm heading back since you handled the situation. Don't be long."

I love that man. "I'll be home soon."

Emerson is staring at the ground, refusing to meet my eyes.

"What are you doing?" I make myself comfortable on the ground.

Her gaze stays downward. "I don't know."

I lay back and glance at the sky. "You do remember

you're married, right?"

Her shoulders sag. "Yes, but we don't even talk. It's so awkward. There is no companionship whatsoever. Before we were married, we were friends. However, the day of the wedding, he changed. He withdrew from everyone and stayed to himself as much as possible."

I'm not surprised. That was the morning I fell to my death and he had to watch. King Percy sure left his mark on him.

She leans back. "The Orlons began visiting the castle again once Sam's engagement to Elizabeth was official. We grew close. I am in a loveless marriage, and he was engaged to someone he couldn't stand. We were in similar situations." She glances at me. "I didn't mean for this to happen. However, I've fallen for him, too."

"Have you tried talking to Nick about it?"

She cringes. "Yes, but he just stayed quiet. He would say he was sorry and walk into his room."

How I wish I could make things right for her, but it's not that easy. "I'm so sorry. I get it, and I promise we will figure this out. However, we have to focus on saving Knova right now."

She giggles. "I wish we had grown up together like this."

I take her hand. "Yes, me too. How were you able to hang around Elizabeth?"

"It wasn't pleasant." She picks at something on her pants. "Everything always had to be her way, and I had to make sure I answered everything the way she wanted."

That makes sense. "I'm sorry you didn't have anyone."

She shrugs. "I had Father. He was there for me a lot."

She glances down at me. "You should give him a chance, similar to how I'm giving Mother a chance. He did do things behind the scenes to protect you all as much as possible."

She's got me there, but what does she mean? I never saw anything like that.

Owen's voice enters my head. *Come on home. We have a big day tomorrow.*

He's right, but that doesn't mean I want to leave. "Hey, I hate to do this, but we both need to get some sleep. I promise, we will figure this all out soon. I want you to be happy."

We both stand, and she smiles. "I'm sure glad I have you. Good night."

She heads back to her house.

As I enter our house, Owen is in the den. "You know I'm not thrilled about your midnight adventure."

I raise an eyebrow. "Good thing you aren't my father. I needed a minute to get away. I didn't expect I'd be walking into that."

He scratches his head. "Yes, you are right, but now, let's go to bed."

We crawl back into bed, and I snuggle into his side.

He leans over and whispers into my ear, "No more escapes tonight. We have a big day tomorrow."

ॐ

WE ARE THE LAST ONES TO WALK INTO THE DINING HALL for breakfast and sit down at the table.

Sam refuses to look at me, while King Michael focuses

on his food, and Queen Lora chats with Mer. That's going to take some time to wrap my head around. Who would have thought they would become friends? I sit beside Lydia.

Smiling, she looks at my plate. "Eat up."

Nick and Emerson are sitting together and not speaking at all, both on the other end of the table away from Sam.

That's good. I want them to be happy and not have anyone causing drama between them.

Claire is staring at her food and moving the eggs around with her fork. She hasn't eaten a bite. Mother is next to her, trying to help. Thank Knova she's back to herself.

Gabe is next to her and keeps looking my way. I sure hope he doesn't try talking to me. I don't have much to say and still need some time to process what Emerson told me last night.

Logan is on Claire's other side, concern etched all over his face and dark circles under his eyes. He keeps watching Claire.

I'm sure it was a long night. Mine was, and my parents weren't at risk.

Owen sits next to me and nudges me, pointing to my food.

Yes, I need to eat. However, I'm not hungry at all. I just want this to be over.

Jacob and Willow move to our side of the table.

"The men are getting ready." Jacob glances at Hazel. "How many will you be able to transport at one time?"

"I will transport as many as needed." She looks at me.

"Do not forget your crown."

Is she being serious? Why in Knova would I wear my crown? I'm going to take down a tyrant, not go to a royal ball. I take a bite of food. "I'll try not to."

Gabe chuckles, and it looks like pride is shining in his eyes.

Yes, this whole thing is strange. I'd rather focus on Marcus instead of attempting to determine my father's motives.

Owen squeezes my leg.

I lean into him. I'm so glad he's mine.

We all focus on eating, and soon, we have no more excuses to sit around. It's time. I glance over and he nods, so we hold hands and stand.

The table becomes quiet when everyone realizes it's time.

I glance at our group. "It's time. Go home and grab anything you need. We will meet at the hunter grounds in fifteen minutes."

Owen and I walk out the door and head home. We grab a bag and put some jerky, nuts, and water into it. The Pearson House is probably stocked, but I doubt we will be there the entire time.

There is a knock at the door.

Who the hell would it be right now? I open the door, and my father comes into view.

What does he want? "Uh... can I help you with something?"

He taps his foot but remains quiet.

Well, this isn't awkward at all.

He forces a grin. "Hey, um... I was hoping we

could talk."

I lean against the door. "Now isn't the best time."

He runs his hands through his hair. "It will just take a second."

I take a step back, not sure what else to do. "Do you want to come in?"

He gives me a relieved smile. "Yes, I'd like that."

I move out of the doorway, and he makes his way into the living room.

Owen looks up. "I need to go get some things out of our room. I'll be right back."

Yeah, leave me, why don't you?

He walks upstairs, but my father stays close to the door.

I can't handle this silence. "You want to discuss something?"

He sighs. "Yes." He looks around and snickers. "Gosh, this is hard, and I don't have a lot of time." He touches my arm. "I want you to know that, despite everything, I love you and Logan. Things got complicated, and my indifference was meant to serve as a form of protection for the two of you."

What? How was it protection?

He walks past me and sits at the kitchen table. "We don't have time, but before we head into a war where anything can happen, I just wanted you to at least hear it from me."

How do I respond to this? Oh, that's okay? Because it wasn't and I'm not going to lie. "Do you know what it was like to be a four-year-old walking past her father and have him not even acknowledge her?"

He takes a deep breath. "I know. I'm sorry, but I had to."

Who the hell does he think he is, coming here now, right before a battle, and saying things like that to me? The table rattles, but I don't even notice it.

Owen comes into the room and looks at my father. "You need to go. You've said what you wanted, but it was just to make you feel better."

Father stands from the table. "No, that's…"

"Yes, that's exactly what it was." He walks to the door and opens it. "I get that you do love her, and I believe you, but you should have waited until after."

I snort. "He doesn't think I'll make it. This was his goodbye."

Father's mouth drops open. "No, that's not it."

Before anything else can happen, there is a strong rattling from upstairs. It sounds like something is trying to break through the floor.

I glance at Owen. "What were you doing upstairs?"

He rolls his eyes at me. "Why would I do something that would cause that?"

I shrug. "I don't know. What the hell is it?"

Father takes a step forward. "Maybe we should check?"

Before we can do much else, there is a crashing down the stairs and the key begins burning around my neck like it used to.

Great, here we go again. The wooden box that holds the crown lands at the bottom of the stairway. I hesitate, and the necklace burns hotter. I guess I'll be going to it.

I bend and open the box then pick up the crown. The key cools off, but the thrumming of the crown takes over.

I don't want to wear this, but it looks as if I don't have much of a choice.

As soon as it's on my head, the thrumming stops as if the last few minutes hadn't happened. I hate this prophecy, but it should end soon. One way or another.

Owen smirks. "I guess Hazel was right when she told you not to forget the crown."

I glare at him. "That's the best you have?"

He walks over and kisses my lips. "Nope, but your father is here, so it's all I've got."

The door opens and in walks Mer. She pauses when she spots my father. "Hey, what's he doing here?"

"He's right here." Father points at himself.

"And talking in third person." She looks at me and places her hand over her mouth, so he can't see it. "That's really weird."

He looks at her, stunned.

Laughter bubbles out of me. I love her. "Don't ever change."

She tosses her hair back. "Don't worry. I won't ever change. Just remember you said this. It will haunt you."

Owen grabs our bags and hands me mine. "Come on, enough goofing off. We have a country to save."

I glare at him. "No pressure at all."

He flexes. "With me by your side, there is no way we can't win."

Mer covers her mouth. "I think I just threw up a little."

Father is watching the exchange and seems to be speechless. That's a change.

I open the door, and we all head out. The closer we get to the hunting grounds, the tenser we all get, even Mer.

Even she realizes how serious the situation is that we are going into.

Jacob is there, along with about thirty of our biggest and toughest men.

He glances behind us. "We are ready once the others arrive."

Logan, Claire, and Mother walk toward us. Looking worse for wear, Claire's eyes are bloodshot and her outfit is in disarray.

I meet her halfway and wrap my arms around her.

She clutches me tighter. "Oh, I'm so upset. I want my parents safe, but I don't want you and Logan to walk into danger. You guys are rushing this because of me."

Why didn't I consider she would think this? "We would never feel one-hundred percent ready for this. And you aren't the reason. If it weren't for your parents, he'd have found something else to get us there. This is not your fault, and you should not feel guilty." I pull back. "Do you understand?"

Tears fill her eyes, but she nods.

I wrap my arms back around her and glance over at Logan.

Logan mouths the words 'thank you' to me.

I wink back at him then pull away, motioning for Mother to take my place. When Logan leaves, it's going to be hard on her, but he's essential for us to win.

She takes my spot, so I head back toward Owen.

The Orlons make their way. Sam is frowning but wearing his battle gear of all black.

King Michael has a sword strapped to his side and a

dagger next to it. I sure hope he doesn't get them confused.

Dressed in all black, Queen Lora has her hair pulled up into a ponytail.

Is she coming with us? "Aren't you staying here?"

"No." She huffs. "Percy betrayed us all, and I won't just sit back and let some backstabber rule my kingdom."

Of course, it's not about the greater good or anything. It's personal to her, but at this point, I'll take what I can get.

Emerson and Nick arrive.

Noslon life seems to agree with Nick. Ever since he came here, he's become more confident and skilled. Even knowing he may face his father, he appears to be ready for battle.

My sister, on the other hand, seems a little more pensive. If she bites her lip any more, I'm afraid it's going to bleed.

Watching her, Sam takes a few steps toward her before making himself stop.

I walk over to her. "Are you okay?"

She pushes a piece of hair behind her ear. "Yes, just a little nervous. This is different than anything I was trained for."

She's right about that. We were trained we would be far behind battle lines, but now, we are at the forefront of it all. Our training did not prepare us for something like this.

The Originals make their way toward us.

Mer points at me. "Look, she didn't forget the crown."

I glare at her.

Shrugging, she points to herself. "Never changing."

I did expect my words to haunt me, but I wasn't expecting it to be so soon.

Willow shifts her bag around. "Let's do this."

Bowing her head, Hazel smiles. "Your crown will help in your endeavors."

Before I can ask any questions, she walks away and opens the portal. The inside of the Pearson house stares back at us.

Gabe walks toward it, but Owen grabs his arm.

I'm not sure what's going on. "I thought you were staying."

Removing Owen's hand, Gabe looks at me. "No, I'm going. You need me. Percy is involved, and unfortunately, I know him better than anyone in this group. He's cruel beyond even what you realize. You need me."

What does that even mean? He isn't aware what all he did to us.

Logan huffs. "We know full well what he is capable of; however, if you want to help us fight, I'm not going to complain."

Can we trust him? I glance at Owen. *Is that wise?*

Owen startles.

I chuckle.

He glances at me. *You don't normally initiate this on purpose. I think we trust him for as long as he allows it. But as soon as we are suspicious, we will take care of it.*

Mer's voice grabs my attention. "Oh, don't worry. She's not going crazy. They are doing their mind-speak thingy."

I ignore her. Whatever I say at this point will be

regretted.

Gabe walks through the portal, and Owen and I follow right behind him.

It's interesting how, in just one step, we've traveled hundreds of miles. Soon, everyone has walked through except for Mother and Claire. They are staying back since they aren't trained for any of this and Claire is too emotionally invested.

We are cramped in this house, so I walk outside, ignoring Owen's protests.

However, once I step foot outside, my breath is stolen away from me. All the trees are dead and sagging. The grass is brown and dead. What the hell happened?

Pierce comes outside with me. "Marcus has taken the essence out of all of the land. I didn't realize how fast he was doing this."

"We have to hurry. We were gone too long."

Owen walks out behind me. "You can't go running off like that."

"I went just a few feet." I motion between us. "You do realize we aren't going to be able to be attached to each other's sides the entire time."

Nick, Logan, Jacob, and Mer walk out, followed by the Noslon hunters that traveled with us.

Standing in front, Owen turns to face them. "Now, the house we need to check out is not far from here. If it's empty, we will need to go around the village undetected and search the palace."

The men nod, and soon, the Orlons and Father walk outside to join us, along with Emerson and the Originals.

Logan moves toward the path. "Let's go."

We travel the short distance to Claire's parents' house, and the front door is wide open. Their land is dried out, and the wind blows dust against the white house.

This isn't good. "I'm going in."

Before Owen can grab me, I'm already several steps ahead. I don't want to go inside this house; I think it's pointless, but I have to check it out.

Logan walks through the door right beside me. The kitchen is in shambles. The dishes are scattered all over the floor, and the kitchen table is broken into several pieces. The chairs are overturned and there is a huge hole in one of the walls.

What the hell happened here?

We walk into the living room, and the couch is over-turned. Derek's favorite chair is broken in half.

Logan runs up the stairs, leaving me behind.

I follow behind, and the walls leading us to her parents' room are all scuffed up. The white sheets have been ripped from the bed and I see a small amount of blood on parts. The side table is overturned and the lamp is broken. Glass is everywhere on the floor.

Logan rushes out, but I can't budge from this spot. My eyes can't leave the blood.

"Ariah." His tone is desperate and loud.

However, I can't leave this room.

Appearing beside me, Owen glares at me. "Don't ever leave me like that again." He glances into the room and follows my gaze then pulls me into his arms. "They are okay. He needs them to get to you. He knows that."

"Get in here now," my brother yells.

Owen pulls me away and into Claire's old room. Her

room looks exactly the same way she had left it. Her clothes are hung up neatly, which must have been her mother's doing, and her bed is made. However, a bloody shirt is laying in the center of the bed. 'I'll see you soon' is written in blood across the front of one of her father's button-up work shirts.

Oh, no. Please, let her parents still be alive. Grace and Derek don't deserve this.

Mer walks into the room and shakes me. "Keep it together. This is what he wants."

Turning, Logan's face is devoid of emotion. "You're right. Let's go. They aren't here."

We walk outside, and Owen tells everyone what we had found.

I can't pay attention, because the bloody shirt keeps haunting me. Whose blood was it? Thank Knova Claire isn't with us.

King Michael is next to me, leaning into my ear. "Pull yourself together. A leader doesn't have time to lose it, and you are their leader today.

I take a deep breath. He's right. I have to force the image from my mind. "Let's head around the village. Be prepared."

Sam walks up next to Emerson, and they walk side by side. At least he's near to protect her.

We walk around the village, but everywhere is death and destruction. All the vegetation is dead, and no one is about like usual.

The entire way to the palace, we don't cross anyone. The few people who are out and about hurry back into their homes.

When we reach the palace gates, we find it deserted. We walk in, but there is no noise, and the staff aren't scurrying around as normal.

The staff are always bustling, so this is strange. When we walk into the palace, we are greeted with complete silence.

Gabe walks to the front and motions us to follow. As we walk through the main corridors and down the hall to the royal chambers, we see nobody. Even the staff is nowhere to be found.

He turns to me. "This isn't right."

He doesn't have to say that more than once. We walk a little further, but nothing else seems out of place, just that the palace is unusually empty and silent.

Jacob hovers near Mer, but she is focused on the threat at hand.

After noting that the palace is empty, we head down toward the dungeon.

Owen and I are following close behind my father, and as soon as we hit the bottom step, the inmates rally.

The cells are full of inmates, all banging on the bars and screaming. When we walk past one housing a younger man with black hair and blue eyes, he holds out a cup. "Please, it's been days since we've had anything to drink."

I set down my bag and pull out a bottle of water. How can I not help them? I open the water and pour some into his cup. But as soon as I do this, another prisoner holds up his cup as well. I go to pour him some when Owen stops me.

He leans close. "Don't give away all your water. There

is no telling how much we'll need."

I get what he is saying, but at this time, these people need it more than me. I pour a little more in the other person's cup and head toward the end of the dungeon.

At the end, where we had met Marcus previously, Dave is still there.

When he sees me, he runs to the cell bars. "I'm so sorry. I never meant to hurt you. Please, help me."

Does he think it will be that easy to regain my favor? "You betrayed me. Do you think I'll be so forgiving?"

He hits his head on the bar. "No, I don't. But I can help you."

Owen focuses on him now. "How?"

Dave meets his gaze. "I've spent time in Crealon, which is where they are from. I can help you."

Hitting the bars, Logan growls. "I don't trust you. You betrayed us."

"I understand your anger and mistrust, but I can be an asset." He grabs the bars. "I know the ins and outs of Crealon."

Owen glances at Jacob, who nods and pulls out some rope.

Pointing to the rope, Owen grins. "Okay, we'll take your help, but you'll be restrained the whole time. We can't take any risks."

Dave takes a big gulp. "Uh, okay."

I want to laugh, but I hold it in. Did he really expect us to just trust him again?

Jacob walks into the cell and roughly ties his hands behind his back. Dave has the good sense not to complain.

I turn toward the others. "They aren't here. We need to

JEN L. GREY

head back to the house and regroup."

We head up the stairs, and Jacob takes up the rear, pulling Dave behind us all.

I want to confront him, but at this point, nothing good can come of it. He would only try to justify his actions, and I would disagree. Why bother having that conversation right now when we have more pressing matters to worry about?

Once more, we head around the town, and still, nothing or nobody bothers us. It's eerily quiet, as if no one lives here.

Soon, we pass Claire's house, and I have to fight to keep the bloody shirt out of my head. We have to reach her parents before it's too late.

Lydia is outside the house when we arrive. "They are gone. We must hurry."

Getting in her face, Logan hits the side of the house beside her head. "Yes, that would have been nice to know a few hours ago."

Pierce walks out the door. "We didn't figure it out until right after you left. Hazel is working on finding a way to get you there quickly."

Concern outlines my brother's face. He glances at me. "Are you okay?"

I take a deep breath. "No, I'm not, but I'll make it through. We have to save them."

Willow runs out the door. "She's figured it out."

Shoving Dave up front, Jacob tightens the ropes. "Make sure we aren't about to run into an ambush."

We walk into the house and find Hazel sitting in the middle of the room. There is a connection here, providing

232

us a view of a place I have never been before. The houses are like no others I have seen. They are sturdy and built into the ground. The tops are made of mud, and the city is all brown.

I look back at Hazel. "Are you sure?"

Dave tenses beside me. "Yes, that's it. Do you see the bigger building surrounded by the rock wall?"

I focus and find a larger house that he must be referring to. It certainly looks to be set apart from the others, even though it sits in the center of the village. "Are you talking about the larger house in the middle?"

He nods. "Yes, that's where Marcus is. It's bigger than it looks."

Mer walks beside me. "That's it? We've got this."

Dave's lips tremble. "Marcus is crazy. Don't underestimate him."

That actually doesn't surprise me. Between the hair and message in blood, he must be. However, we don't have time to worry about it. Too much is at stake.

"Hazel, please open up the connection."

She looks at me and bows her head. "Give me two minutes."

Jacob walks over to Mer. "You need to stay close."

She pulls out her dagger. "Like hell I do."

Now is not the time for him to become all domineering. "Mer, will you help me keep an eye on our prisoner? I don't trust him."

Jacob gives me a thankful look, but I ignore it. I don't want to deal with their games.

The room seems to be expanding. Hazel must be ready for us to cross. I just hope we all make it back.

Chapter Fifteen

Owen grabs my hand and looks at me. "Are you ready?"

I nod. I'm as ready as I'm ever going to be.

We both walk toward the image and are transported there. Just like in Agrolon, it doesn't appear that anyone is out and about.

Jacob and Mer follow us, and soon, the Orlons, Nick, Emerson, and the thirty hunters are here.

I'm about to step away when Pierce comes through as well. I didn't expect him to come with us.

I'm making my way toward the large building in the center when I see guards come into view.

They are large and suited up in what looks to be some sort of armor. However, the material moves with them and fits their bodies like a second skin.

How are we going to compete with that?

They attack us with long swords, and our hunters use their own swords to hold them back.

However, it's a tough fight. Their swords are more slender than ours, but they are still making more of an impact. How is that possible?

Pierce moves toward Owen and me. "I'll be right back."

Before we can say anything, he disappears from sight.

Owen glances at me. "I guess he wasn't asking."

Before we can say much more, Ares comes up beside me.

What the hell? How is this possible. "Hey, what are you doing here?"

He neighs and heads off to the woods bordering their central area. If you could call them woods. The trees are all dead and sagging, even worse than the vegetation in the other kingdoms.

Mer comes over, pulling Dave behind her. "He's in the big house."

Huh? "How do you know that?"

She exhales. "Because he is very strong. I can see his power's signature from here."

Pierce comes back. "He knows we are here. I couldn't get close enough, but he is using these guards as a distraction. He wants to see how smart you are."

Well, I had hoped not to make a scene, but at this point, we're going to need to. I take Owen's hand. *Should we just go for it?*

He grins. *I'm finally rubbing off on you. Let's make some noise.*

I glance around and find Emerson, Sam, and Logan a few feet over.

King Michael and Nick are with the hunters, engaged in battle.

I run over to my sister and brother. "Are you guys ready to end this? I'm tired of dragging this out."

She nods and takes a step toward me.

Sam grabs her wrist and looks at me. "Can't you do this without her?"

Logan glares at him. "Do you think I want either of my sisters in this? But, as always, this is our family's curse."

Removing his hand, she gives Sam a sad smile. "I'm sorry, but I have to go. This is my destiny. I couldn't live with myself if I didn't." She kisses his cheek. "I'm done being afraid."

She walks off to the others with Logan by her side.

Sam is devastated.

I touch his arm. "I'll take care of her. I promise." I turn to walk away.

"Ari." His tone is quiet, desperation leaking through.

I glance back.

He sighs. "Please, keep her safe. Even if we have no future together, I want her to be okay."

He does love her. I nod and head back to the group. I'll do anything in my power to keep all of them safe

Gabe is now there with the rest of my crew.

Mer grins. "I hear we are about to have some fun."

Of course she'd think it was fun. "No, we are about to head straight into harm's way."

"You say harm." She points at herself. "I say fun."

Jacob is frowning, and his arms are crossed. "This isn't a game. That's why you'll be stuck with me."

She pushes her finger into his chest. "I can take care of myself. I don't need you hovering."

Are they arguing over this right now? "Okay, Mer can

tell that he is in fact at the large house. So, that's where we are heading."

I look at Dave. "You lead the way. You know this place better than anyone." Glancing at Mer again, I point to her. "I want you to stay close to him."

Owen motions to Jacob. "You take the front to cover Mer and Dave, and I'll take the back. Logan and Emerson, you two stay close to Ariah."

"I'll go around and check the perimeter," Pierce volunteers and takes off.

It's crazy how fast he can move. It's like he was just there and disappeared.

"What about me?" Father is looking at us for direction.

I don't trust him and don't want him going with us. "Why don't you stay here? The hunters are having a hard time holding off the guards. They could use the help."

He pinches the bridge of his nose. "I will not stay here while all of my children go head-first into danger."

Owen rubs my arm. "That's fine, you can stay with me."

I want to argue, but time is of the essence.

Jacob takes off, and Mer and Dave follow close behind.

Grabbing my arm, Logan puts himself between Emerson and me. We go to the right, away from the other guardsmen. I'm sure this is what Marcus wants, but right now, we're going to let him think we are playing into his hands.

Dave is taking the lead, and I hope we aren't making a mistake by trusting him.

As we move through the alleyways and pass a group of houses, people peek out their windows, just watching us walk by. Why are all the residents staying in their homes? You'd think they would be out helping the guards or causing an uprising.

The entire way, we run into no problems, and when we reach the large house, Pierce materializes beside me.

Jacob checks to make sure nobody is behind us, and then we all take a second to catch our breath.

This is it. There is no turning back. If we don't win, Knova will fall into the hands of evil. It's almost like that now.

Once we're ready, Jacob opens the door and we all follow him inside Marcus's lair.

The room is so dark that it's almost as if we are blind. I hold out my hand and push my power out, materializing a small fireball in the palm of my hand.

Gabe's eyes widen. "Is that smart?"

"Maybe not." I hold my hand out to lighten the whole room. "But we can't see without it. Is it better to be blind or have some visibility?"

I move to go to the front of our group.

Owen grabs my waist. "Where do you think you're going?"

Is he being serious right now? Someone has to lead the way, and no one else is using their power. "I'm going up front, so Dave can lead the way." I twist out of his grasp and walk to the front.

Jacob steps up beside me. "Let's go." He leads us down a long hallway until it splits into three paths, making him pause.

"What's wrong?" I look down each path. "Why'd you stop?"

Sighing, he turns to me. "I don't know which way he is."

"Seriously? What good are you?" Mer closes her eyes, and when she opens them, her jade eyes are glowing just like Willow's. "He's down this way." She points to the right then walks down the hall, leaving us behind.

Jacob rushes past me. "What the hell? Wait for the rest of us."

We follow her down the path until we reach a steep stairway leading up to another level. She pauses and looks at each of us. "He's up there."

Dave steps back and bumps into Owen.

Glowering, Owen shoves him. "What the hell are you doing?"

He tries to pass him again. "Hey, I've done my part. I got you here. I'm out."

Annoyed, my father looks at him in disgust. "Just let him go. He's useless anyway."

Owen grabs him by the shirt and pushes him forward. "Oh, no, he's staying with us. I don't trust him otherwise."

Walking past us, Logan takes the stairs. "Let's just get this over with."

We all fall in line behind him, walking up at least one hundred stairs. When we reach the landing at the top, there is an arched wooden door.

Grabbing the steel door handle, Logan pushes it open.

We enter the door and find ourselves on one side of the top level of the house. It's all outside up here. We have a view of the entire kingdom.

Stepping out onto the roof's floor, we all fan out and take in the view. The woods here are in worse shape than the ones in Agrolon. These woods are black and decaying, and the smell of rot in the air is overwhelming.

"Isn't it beautiful?"

Marcus's voice startles me. I turn and find him admiring the sickly view I was just looking at.

Trembling, Emerson takes a step toward the ledge. "The forest is dead."

Marcus's face morphs into a huge smile. "I know. It's all my handy work."

Pierce's face is horrified. "How could you? This is beyond cruel."

"Oh, brother, I only started out wanting to be powerful like our sisters. But I realized how much more I can be." He chuckles. "I can be more powerful than them all, and I will be once the Savior is dead." His eyes flicker to me.

He's crazy. Why else would he be doing this? "Why can't we just work together? No one person has to rule over the country."

He rubs his bottom lip. "You see, I do have to rule over everything in order to prove that I'm the strongest."

Owen's power is thrumming due to his rising anger. "But you aren't truly the strongest. You're manipulating the elements for your power, for it to appear that way. It's not natural."

He shrugs. "Who cares? As long as I'm the strongest, it doesn't matter."

He's like a spoiled child, thinking he deserves the bigger piece of cake or the most toys. There is no rationalizing with him.

His body tenses. "What the hell is that?"

I glance in the direction he is looking and find a small patch of green bleeding through the black. What's going on?

He rushes to the edge of the landing as more green appears.

The green is getting closer to the village when Ares appears, staring right up at us.

Am I seeing things or is Ares helping the forest somehow?

Marcus turns to me, hatred clear on his face. "It's time to end this."

With no other warning, he throws power at me.

I jump to the side, barely missing the force of the blow he just hurled in my direction.

Owen rushes next to me and throws power back at him.

However, Marcus shields himself, causing it to bounce back toward Mer.

Jacob jumps in front of her, taking the blast.

She screams, but he is now just lying on the floor, not moving.

Marcus uses my distraction and shifts the air around me, placing me in the middle of a small tornado.

I call for my power and grab at the wind surrounding me, making it still.

Owen pulls out his sword and goes for Marcus, striking his arm, but Marcus turns around and uses the air to slam him into the wall.

I want to run to him and check on him, but now is not the time. Logan and Emerson take their place on either side of me. I reach out and connect with them, needing this battle to end.

Blood is running down Marcus's arm, but his eyes are still on me. He lifts his head, and fire surrounds us.

Of course, it'd be fire, because water is my weakest connection. Don't think like that, I got this. I ask the water to come to me and focus on drenching the fire surrounding us. I push my power into Emerson, who causes the ground underneath him to shake.

He's still standing on the edge, so Emerson pushes more power into the ground. The railing breaks off, sending Marcus over the edge.

I break our connection, and Owen rushes over to look down.

Could it be that easy? Are we done?

Mer's frantic voice captures my attention. "Ariah, I need you here now."

I turn and find Mer hovered over Jacob, and he still isn't moving. Rushing to him, I find that the power had struck his chest, right where his heart is.

She grabs my arm, pulling me down. "Fix him, please. He can't die."

He's breathing, so it's worth a shot.

I put my hands over his wounds, the blood sticky against my fingers. I almost gag at the metallic scent assaulting my senses. I focus on his chest and picture his chest healing, pushing my power into him.

"It's not working." Mer's voice shakes.

I don't think I've ever healed this bad of wound before, except for that time I was poisoned, but I had Owen... yes, Owen. *I need you. He isn't healing fast enough.*

Owen's arms surround me, and he places his head on my neck. I reach out and merge with him, and his power fills me. I push even more into Jacob and imagine his wound closing.

I don't know how long I stay like this, but Jacob's voice knocks me out of my concentration. "I'm good. I'm good. Thank you."

I lift my head to find Jacob staring at me. Pulling my hands away from his chest, I wipe them on my pants.

Jacob sits up and wobbles a little.

Mer throws herself into his lap. "Don't you ever do something so stupid again."

"There was no way I was going to let that hit you."

Before he can say another word, Mer puts her mouth on his.

He doesn't move for a second, but soon, he's kissing her back with fervor.

Well, I guess a near-death experience got them on the same page.

Owen tugs me into him. "He's not dead. We have to go. He was making his way out to the forest."

Nodding, Pierce points to the forest. "He's after Ares."

Gabe is standing still in one place.

Concerned, Emerson tugs on his arm. "Are you okay?"

He gazes at me. "I can't believe what I just saw. You can heal people."

"Yes, I can." If he had been around, he might have already known that. "But right now, we need to get out to the forest."

Jacob pulls away from Mer. "Yes, we need to get going. We aren't safe here."

Owen opens the door. "Everyone, stay alert. Marcus is unpredictable, so there is no telling what may be in store for us."

I follow him down the stairs and light the fireball in my hand again, leading the way. Once we are outside, we head toward the green. As we walk past the homes, the hunters, Nick, King Michael, and Queen Lora come into view. They are struggling but still holding their ground.

Owen glances back. "We need to hurry. They are outnumbered and won't last much longer."

Finding the green is easy in a sea of rotting black and decay. When we come upon Marcus, he has Ares by the neck.

Who the hell does he think he is? He's hurt too many to get away with this. Without thinking, I reach out and attempt to connect with my power, but it's so low from healing Jacob that there isn't anything to grab. What the hell am I going to do?

Marcus' cruel grins spreads across his face. "You really thought you were going to win, didn't you?"

Struggling to breathe, the stallion is no longer fighting as hard.

He's going to die if I don't do something. I rush toward him, just needing to distract Marcus.

Owen's voice rings loud behind me. "What the hell are you doing?" He's running to catch up behind me.

Don't overthink this. I jump on Marcus' back and pull at his hair.

Laughing, Marcus moves his hand and throws me on the ground right in front of Owen.

Owen grabs me and pulls me to my feet. 'Don't you

ever do something like that again."

He thinks now is the time to lecture me? And he thinks I have problems.

Logan rushes Marcus.

Marcus throws him down on the ground behind me. "This is so much fun." He smirks at me. "What's wrong? You've run your power low?"

He shifts the ground up from underneath me.

It's shifting and turning and much to my horror, the ground is opening up. Before I can move, I'm tumbling down ten feet and land in a dark, narrow musky hole. The crown on my head begins falling off, and I grab it and place it back upright.

At my touch, the crown on my head buzzes to life at the connection. Its own energy pulses into me and replenishes mine.

Thank Knova. I call to the ground underneath me and lift myself back up to the others.

When I appear, Marcus frowns at my appearance. "How the hell did you do that?"

Owen rushes over to me. "Are you okay?"

I nod. "I'm fine, but we don't have time for this."

He frowns at me, but I ignore him.

I reach my power out to connect with him, Logan, and Emerson. The connection is stronger than ever thanks to the crown on top of my head.

Glaring at Marcus, I force all the power out of me at one time, aiming at his heart.

When it hits, he flies into the air and lands on a decaying tree branch that easily punctures his body. The leafy, green branch is sticking through his chest.

Ares stumbles back and straightens to his full height.

Thank Knova my stallion friend is okay.

Pierce runs over to his brother, tears in his eyes. "If only you had continued to love nature and the elements that connect us all, then your end wouldn't have had to be this way. Greed took over, and for that, you must pay your dues. Until we meet again."

Blood dribbles down the dying Original's mouth. "This isn't over. I'm strong. I'll find a way back." Then his eyes glaze over and he stops moving.

Pierce waves his hands over his brother. "He is dead." Then his brother vanishes from sight, disappearing into thin air.

I walk over and hug Pierce. "I'm so sorry."

He returns the embrace. "No, I'm sorry. You shouldn't have had to go through all this."

Mer walks over to where Marcus was. "What happened to him?"

"When an Original dies, we bless them so they can become one with nature again." Pierce stares at the place his brother was moments ago.

Tapping her lips, Mer grins. "I bet he doesn't appreciate that. Serves him right."

Owen wraps his arm around me. "Are you okay?"

"No, but I will be."

Logan moves back toward the village. "As touching as all this is, we need to get back and help the others."

Nodding, Emerson rushes back that way.

I bet she is worried about Sam.

We all follow, and when we reach the others, they are barely holding the guards off. I connect the four of us, the crown adding energy, and I push the guards away. "Marcus is dead. You don't have to fight us any longer."

The guard in front, who must be the leader, stares at me and bows.

I glance over and find Emerson grinning.

"What's going on?"

She giggles. "Your crown. It's shining."

The guard rises. "You have the crown of the Savior. If we had known, we wouldn't have fought you."

Sam moves to stand next to Emerson, and the hunters put down their swords.

I raise my head. "Good, then please go fetch the prisoners that Marcus was keeping from Agrolon."

The guard nods, and they leave to do my bidding.

Nick is standing by the forest, very tense, and there is blood streaking his face. His eyes are wild.

I walk over to him. "Are you okay?"

He looks behind me. "Go now."

Before another word leaves my mouth, I'm tugged back against someone, and a dagger is at my throat.

King Percy's orange scent infiltrates my nose. The dagger is piercing my skin. "Good job, son. Maybe there is some hope for you after all."

Taking a menacing step toward us, Owen growls. "Let her go now."

He pushes the dagger a little more into my neck, and I feel a thin line of blood flowing from the wound. "No, I will be the ruler. I will kill the Savior and become the ruler of all."

He grabs my face, turning it toward him, his smirk on full display. "This is over now."

He tightens his hold, but before I can react, he goes limp.

I rush out of his arms and turn to find that Nick has stabbed his father right through the heart.

The King collapses before my eyes.

Nick is trembling as he watches the life leave his father.

Glancing at me, his face is full of remorse. "I'm so sorry. I should have never let you go. I was such a coward."

My eyes can't stay on him. They keep finding Percy laying there on the ground, dead.

Before he can finish his apology, Elizabeth comes out of the forest and walks up behind us. She rushes at Nick.

What the hell? I glance back at him and move to help, but she has already slit his throat. "You are pathetic, brother."

"No." I'm hoping there is something I can do, but in my heart, I know I'm too late.

She charges at me, but I still can't get past Nick bleeding out right in front of me.

Pierce appears before me and breaks her neck.

Her eyes widen before she falls to her death beside her brother and father.

There is so much death and destruction around me. How did this become my life? Tears cloud my vision, but I take a deep breath and hold my head up high.

The main guard appears with a beaten-up Derek and Grace in tow. I make my way to them and give them both a hug. They may be beaten, but at least they are alive.

Logan comes up next to me, taking my place to hug

them. They are asking about Claire, but my brain has had all it can take.

I walk to Owen and wrap my arms around him. "I'm ready to go home."

We walk back to the portal where we had entered.

My mate turns back. "Jacob, will you stay back here and figure out a plan with the Crealons? We can't leave them high and dry."

He nods, and Owen takes me back home.

Epilogue

✿

It's midnight, and I'm standing at the water's edge in Noslon. I have nightmares of that day in Crealon, and once again, the horrific scenes woke me up tonight. How I wish Nick was alive. I rub the scar on my neck that serves as the constant reminder of that day.

People keep promising things will get better, but I don't think they ever will. There are some things that can't be justified, no matter the outcome.

Owen sits beside me on the ground. "More bad dreams?"

I scoot closer to him. "Yes, I'm sorry. They just won't go away."

He wraps his arm around my waist. "At least we have each other."

I grin. "That's true."

"Your sister is going to be upset with you. Tomorrow is her and Sam's wedding."

I sigh. "Yes, and this time, I'll get to attend it."

"At least you don't have to watch her kiss someone all the time." He shakes his head. "I don't understand why Mer has to be all over Jacob wherever they go."

And she used to say we were bad. "I'm happy for them."

"Yes, I'm happy for them, too, but...," he shudders, "she's my sister. I shouldn't be subjected to that."

"At least it's just your sister." I tap his nose. "I have to watch my father and mother be like that. Now, that's gross."

He chuckles. "Well, we are now the rulers of Knova. We can decree anything we want." He winks at me.

I giggle. That may be the case, but we don't act like the rulers. We lead the country like the Noslon village has always been run. We do the work and blend in with everybody else, except when hard decisions are needed.

The Orlons are still led by King Michael and Queen Lora, and Agrolon will be led by Emerson and Sam. Claire and Logan have taken up residence in Crealon, and we have made them the rulers there.

I try not to visit Crealon, for there are too many bad memories. Although, Claire found a brown stone from there that fit my crown perfectly. I guess that was the intent all along, to have a stone from each kingdom.

However, it's nice that my father and I have finally connected. The reason for his indifference was due to all the extra beatings Logan and I would get if he paid us too much attention or tried to help us behind the scenes. So, our beatings weren't just for us. They served as a reminder for him to keep his distance. It still hurts that he wasn't around, but knowing he was trying to protect us the best he could, given the situation, has thawed my heart a little. Owen's is a whole different story.

Owen stands and grabs my hand. "Come on, princess. Let's go to bed."

৩১৫৩

THE END

৩১৫৩

Check out my future projects at my website.
www.jenlgrey.com

৩১৫৩

Sign up for my newsletter!

About the Author

Jen L. Grey is a new, indie author who focuses on YA fantasy and paranormal genres.

Jen lives in Tennessee with her husband, two daughters, and toy Australian Shephard. Before she started writing, she was an avid reader and enjoyed being involved in the indie community. Her love for books eventually led her to writing and running a blog with one of her close friends. For more information, please visit her website and sign up for her newsletter.

Also by Jen L. Grey

THE PEARSON PROPHECY

Dawning Ascent

Enlightened Ascent

Reigning Ascent